AVON'S VELVET GLOVE SERIES

"THE VELVET GLOVE SERIES WILL BECOME AN EXCITING ALTERNATIVE TO THE STRAIGHT ROMANCE. ALL OF THE SENSUALITY AND MAGNETISM OF ROMANCES IS THERE AND ALSO THE 'CLIFF-HANGING' TENSENESS OF GOOD SUSPENSE."

Affaire de Coeur

"IT'S WHAT WE FEEL IS A NEW TREND IN ROMANTIC FICTION—ROMANTIC SUSPENSE."

Kathryn Falk,
Romantic Times

"THE VELVET GLOVE LINE IS GEARED TO ROMANTIC SUSPENSE... THE SURVIVAL OF LOVE HOLDS THE READER IN AS MUCH SUSPENSE AS THE DANGER."

Terri Busch,
Heart Line

Avon Books publishes two new Velvet Glove books each month. Ask for them at your bookstore.

Other Books in the
Velvet Glove Series:

THE VENUS SHOE *by Carla Neggers*
CAPTURED IMAGES *by Laurel Winslow*
DANGEROUS ENCHANTMENT *by Jean Hager*
THE WILDFIRE TRACE *by Cathy Gillen Thacker*
IN THE DEAD OF THE NIGHT *by Rachel Scott*
THE KNOTTED SKEIN *by Carla Neggers*
LIKE A LOVER *by Lynn Michaels*
THE HAUNTED HEART *by Barbara Doyle*
FORBIDDEN DREAMS *by Jolene Prewit-Parker*
TENDER BETRAYAL *by Virginia Smiley*
FIRES AT MIDNIGHT *by Marie Flasschoen*

Avon Books are available at special quantity discounts for bulk purchases for sales promotions, premiums, fund raising or educational use. Special books, or book excerpts, can also be created to fit specific needs.

For details write or telephone the office of the Director of Special Markets, Avon Books, Dept. FP, 1790 Broadway, New York, New York 10019, 212-399-1357.

Velvet Glove 3

Betty Henrichs
Love's Suspect

AVON
PUBLISHERS OF BARD, CAMELOT, DISCUS AND FLARE BOOKS

LOVE'S SUSPECT is an original publication of Avon Books. This work has never before appeared in book form. This work is a novel. Any similarity to actual persons or events is purely coincidental.

AVON BOOKS
A division of
The Hearst Corporation
1790 Broadway
New York, New York 10019
Copyright © 1984 by Denise Marcil & Meredith Bernstein
Published by arrangement with Velvet Glove, Inc.,
Library of Congress Catalog Card Number: 84-91100
ISBN: 0-380-88013-X

All rights reserved, which includes the right to reproduce this book or portions thereof in any form whatsoever except as provided by the U. S. Copyright Law. For information address Meredith Bernstein, Literary Agent, 33 Riverside Drive, New York, New York 10023 or Denise Marcil Literary Agency, 316 West 82nd Street, New York, New York 10024

First Avon Printing, August, 1984

AVON TRADEMARK REG. U. S. PAT. OFF. AND IN OTHER COUNTRIES, MARCA REGISTRADA, HECHO EN U. S. A.

Printed in the U. S. A.

WFH 10 9 8 7 6 5 4 3 2 1

To Kent, whose love, support, and knowledge
made this book possible.

LOVE'S SUSPECT

Chapter One

WHITNEY'S smile was deliberately confident as she walked into the restaurant of Stanringham's department store to keep her appointment with Bradford Prescott. As she followed the waiter to a secluded table she caught a glimpse of herself in one of the ornate mirrors decorating the walls. She noted with satisfaction that her apricot linen suit was attractively professional. Her leather briefcase spoke of success. Yes, the image was perfect, she decided as the waiter pulled out the plush chair for her. Her carefully cultivated aura of assurance drew more than one appreciative glance from the lunching businessmen. They didn't see the slight tremble of her hand when she smoothed back her ebony hair.

The minutes crawled. She hated waiting! Whitney glanced impatiently at her watch, then pulled from her briefcase the computer printout of Stanringham's inventory. She was making notes in the margin when a rich baritone voice commented, "Such dedication. You don't even know if you've gotten the job yet, Ms. Wakefield, and already you're hard at work."

Whitney glanced up and blinked. She gripped her pencil more tightly as sensations she hadn't felt for two years swirled through her. Thick hair, the color of ripened wheat; eyes the mysterious grayed-green of an olive leaf; high cheekbones she suddenly yearned to reach up and touch; an uncompromisingly square chin softened by a dimple . . . the inventory might have gone on endlessly, because she somehow sensed she would never tire of looking at him. His question finally recalled her senses.

"You are Whitney Wakefield, aren't you?"

"Yes, indeed." She gave herself a hard mental shake to gather her wits as she placed her hand in his. "And are you Mr. Prescott?"

Bradford nodded, then grinned. "I hate formal introductions, don't you?" he commented, seating himself without letting go of her hand. "It reminds me of the dancing school my mother made me go to when I was ten."

"You don't sound like you enjoyed it."

"I didn't!"

"I can't imagine why not. I'll bet all the little girls fought to dance with you."

"You'd lose that bet. At ten I was shorter than most of the girls in my class and wore thick glasses. I was most definitely the wallflower type."

She couldn't keep her eyes from roaming over the strong contours of his face again. Without thinking she murmured, "What happened?"

His deep laugh echoed through the room. "I grew and got contacts." Suddenly his expression became more serious. His grasp tightened around her fingers. "I hope you approve of the change."

The air around them crackled with a tingling awareness as their eyes locked. A magnetism she'd never experienced before was physically drawing them together. She knew from the flash in his eyes that he was feeling it as strongly as she. In that perfect moment it seemed as if they were the only two people in the world.

She was the first to recover. Reluctantly she pulled her hand from his. "Mr. Prescott, I've been studying your computer system and—"

"Whitney," he interrupted, "my name is Bradford. If we're going to be working closely together for several weeks on a new computer program for Stanringham's inventory control, I don't want any of this 'Mr.' and 'Ms.' nonsense between us."

She smiled. The prospect of spending those weeks with the vice-president of Stanringham's was looking more inviting by the moment. Now all she had to do was convince him to give her the contract. "That will make it more comfortable . . . Bradford."

He flashed a boyish smile that tugged at her heart.

Love's Suspect

"Let's order some lunch and then discuss your concepts for redesigning the store's computer system."

After they'd finished the veal scallopini and fresh fruit salad, Whitney tried to resist dessert, but Bradford refused to listen. "I want you to try it. The raspberry mousse is Stanringham's speciality. Besides," he commented letting his gaze trail suggestively over her trim figure, "from what I can tell the extra calories won't hurt. I'll say one thing: meeting you sure destroys one stereotype. Who would have guessed someone who programs computers for a living would turn out to be such a beautiful woman! Maybe I should give the contract to someone else. You could prove to be too much of a distraction!"

Whitney's back stiffened as she met his gaze. She'd felt drawn to Bradford from the moment they'd met, but if he was just another guy out for a tumble her instincts had misfired. She wasn't idiotic enough to wish that her appearance would not attract men's attention. She'd taken special care today with her masses of dark hair, and she remembered that Douglas, in one of his rare poetic moments, had compared her dark eyes to pools of black velvet. But if that was *all* a man saw, *all* he was interested in, then she wasn't interested in him. Respect for her mind, respect for her abilities—that's what held more importance.

A hint of the irritation crackling inside her sharpened her voice. "You may not think I look like a computer programmer, but that's what I am—and I'm a darned good one. Since that's the reason I'm here, don't you think we should drop the personal comments and get back to business?"

A flush of embarrassment darkened Bradford's face. "Whitney, I'm sorry. That must have sounded like the usual macho line. I don't know what it is," he admitted with a shake of his head that loosened a lock of blond hair. "I looked at you and suddenly things were coming out of my mouth I didn't expect."

He paused, his eyes growing serious. "I want one thing understood right now. You're a professional and that's the way you're going to be treated. If you get this contract it will be because of your ideas and your qualifications." He held out his hand and smiled. "Agreed?"

"Sounds fair enough." She nodded, putting her hand in

his for the confirming shake. As their touch lingered, she looked into his eyes, and the smile slipped easily back onto her lips. Watch it! a warning voice whispered. Any man who can melt away your irritation with just a look is dangerous. But the sensations stirred by his fingers curling around hers made her deaf.

Reluctantly Whitney pulled her hand away, determined to get back to business. "Now for those qualifications you mentioned—or, I should confess, the lack of them. This is the first independent assignment that Mr. Greenwald has given me since I started working for Your Program Place. I haven't been with his company very long."

Abruptly she stopped. For an instant her eyes slid away from his. Her fingers tightened around the handle of her coffee cup as the bitter memories of the job she'd had before coming to Your Program Place tried to surface. No! She'd put the past behind her and, damn it, that's where it was going to stay.

Whitney forced her voice to remain blandly neutral as she continued, wanting to convince Bradford the hesitation meant nothing. "Since this is my first solo job, it's vitally important to my career that I succeed."

"I wouldn't worry about that. I've dealt with Mr. Greenwald before. He's as hard-nosed as they come, but he only hires the best. Let's hear your ideas."

Whitney shoved her raspberry mousse aside and spread the computer printout on the table. "I've been studying your present computer system, and I've found several areas where I think things can be changed to give you better inventory control."

For the next hour they drank coffee and talked about what Stanringham's needed in a new computer program. The words were all about business, inventory control, and programming, yet the attraction flaring between them colored every sentence, made every pause seem intimate. No man had ever affected her this way, not even Douglas, and it put her off balance. She glanced at Bradford through the dark fringe of her lashes, remembering his earlier admission. Whatever was happening between them, at least she wasn't struggling with the confusion alone.

He caught her look and smiled. "I'll bet you're wondering if I'll ever run out of questions. Well, I have, and I'm

Love's Suspect 13

satisfied. The boss, Morgan Stanringham, wanted me to write this program myself, but now I'm glad I didn't have the time. I think you'll do an excellent job. Shall we go to my office and sign the contract?"

Whitney sighed with relief. "I can't think of anything I'd rather do."

As they walked through the store on the way to Bradford's office Whitney could see why Stanringham's was called the finest department store in St. Louis. An aura of opulence hovered over everything. The floors were marble, and plush Oriental rugs lay underfoot between the aisles. In one area the clink of champagne glasses mixed with the softly humming cash register as well-dressed shoppers thronged around a designer trunk showing. In another department a striking blond model pirouetted, showing off a chinchilla coat for a customer. Even the stereo equipment and televisions were uniquely displayed in individual room settings.

The executive offices were as elegantly appointed as the rest of the store. Bradford paused outside a teak door, and Whitney stopped beside him, lightheaded from his closeness. Without thinking, she made a move to open his office door. Her hand dropped to the doorknob at the same time he reached for it. His hand closed over hers. The touch sent a wave of desire through Whitney, heating her blood, startling her by the intensity of the feeling.

"No matter what I do I always seem to end up holding your hand. Do you suppose it's fate?"

"Fate or a smooth technique, I'm not sure which," she teased softly, finding it very difficult to breathe with him standing so closely beside her. "I guess I won't object, just as long as you let go of my hand long enough for me to sign that contract."

"Business! Is that all you ever think about?" he laughed, pushing open the office door. "Okay, let's get those papers signed. They're on my desk."

As he moved across his spacious office Bradford continued to talk about some of the special features the computer system needed. Whitney didn't hear a word he said. Her eyes were riveted to his unusual kidney-shaped rosewood desk; a desk that was so familiar . . . so mesmerizing with the shocking memories it brought back. In an instant she was swept back two years to San Francisco.

It all seemed so vivid, flashing through her mind. Mr. Cramer, president of American Securities, had been sitting like a judge behind a desk like Bradford's when the five cashiers walked into his office. Whitney could still hear his condemning voice as he'd accused, "Our courier carrying the four million dollars in bearer bonds was robbed this morning. Only you five people knew where he'd be when. One of you is guilty as hell! The police are waiting outside."

A racking tremor snaked up her back as Whitney remembered the nightmare of those weeks. The endless hours of being questioned by the police, the S.E.C. investigation, the silent accusation in Douglas's eyes, the lie detector tests which cleared no one, the days of waiting and praying for the real thief to be caught, the feeling of helplessness, knowing she was innocent, yet being unable to prove it. Like a whirlpool the investigation had sucked her in deeper and deeper. Now she couldn't pull her eyes away from Bradford's desk as the agony of that final day stabbed through her mind.

Like an executioner, Mr. Cramer had summoned the five back to his office. His words pounded in her head again. "One of you has been clever enough not to leave a trail. The police have no leads. The man from the New York Stock Exchange was here today, and he gave me no choice. You're all fired! None of you will ever work for a brokerage firm again."

Whitney was innocent, yet the stigma of guilt branded her nonetheless. Her past followed her even now like a haunting ghost since the real thief had never been caught.

Vaguely, as if from a far distance, she felt Bradford's concerned touch upon her arm. "Whitney, what's wrong? You look . . . Are you all right?"

The sound of his voice, his obvious concern, pulled her back to the present and helped her yank a shutter down on the memories. She brushed the dark hair away from her face and summoned a smile.

Her smile didn't fool him. His look searched her dark eyes. "Whitney, what happened? For a moment there you looked . . . as if you were afraid of something."

"Afraid? The only thing I'm afraid of is failure. I hate to admit it, but seeing that contract lying on your desk triggered a good old-fashioned attack of nerves. I guess I'm more uptight about tackling my first independent assignment than I thought."

She read doubt in his expression, but she couldn't tell him the truth. The past was gone. The determined tilt of her chin spoke eloquently of her resolve not to let the past hurt her ever again. Her step was steady as she walked across to Bradford's desk and picked up the contract. "Do you have a pen or shall I dig around in my purse for one?"

He took the gold pen from his shirt pocket. "Here, use this. Then we can toast the contract with some coffee."

"What? No champagne?" she laughed, boldly scrawling her name across the bottom of the contract.

He signed below, then looked up at her. A fire kindled in his eyes, turning them the color of jade. "The office is no place for savoring champagne. I think we'll save that for other celebrations."

He didn't add, "more private celebrations," but the message was clear in the way he looked at her. The sense of tantalizing awareness that seemed to blaze every time their eyes met enveloped Whitney again. Her heart beat faster. Bradford slowly straightened and took a step toward her. Both jumped when a sharp rap on the door shattered the moment.

Bradford smiled. "You see, I told you the office wasn't the place for drinking champagne. We'd have been interrupted before the first sip." He raised his voice. "Come in."

A hefty man with graying red hair strode into the room. He wore chocolate brown coveralls with *Stanringham's* neatly emblazoned in gold across the pocket.

"Charlie, you're just the man I was going to call. I'd like you to meet Ms. Whitney Wakefield. She's going to be redoing our computer system."

Charlie's head bobbed as he vigorously shook her hand. "Pleased to meet you, ma'am. You're mighty pretty to be spending your days sitting behind a computer."

"I should've warned you, Whitney; Charlie's the biggest charmer in the store." Bradford smiled affectionately at the older man. "He's also the best maintenance manager in St. Louis. That's why we put up with his blarney."

Charlie winked at her. "Blarney? Since when is telling the truth blarney? You are pretty enough to be a model," he complimented Whitney before settling down to business. "I suppose you need me to rustle up an office for Ms. Wakefield. There's one vacant in the buyer's section, or we can—"

"All I really need is a desk," she interrupted. "Is there room to put one right in the computer room? That would make it a lot easier."

Charlie scratched his head. "Sure, I can do that, but it won't be very elegant."

"I'll take convenience over elegance any day."

"If you ever need anything," Bradford noted, "don't hesitate to call Charlie. He has keys to everything and can get you any supplies you need."

"You can call just to chat too!" Charlie winked at her again, before turning to Bradford. "Almost forgot why I came busting in here. Those fancy display cases Miss Hopper ordered to show off her furs just arrived. I swear, that woman gets more scatterbrained every year. She had them sent C.O.D. instead of invoiced the usual way. Can you believe that? Anyway, I need you to write a check for them."

After Charlie was gone, Bradford smiled. "Now for that coffee I promised." He punched the intercom. "Martha, would you please have some coffee sent up?"

In a crisply efficient voice, his secretary replied, "If you want coffee, I'll have to send it to Mr. Stanringham's office. He just called and would like to meet with you and Ms. Wakefield immediately."

Morgan Stanringham's office was an antique-lover's delight, with ornate Empire furniture and an authentic Bukhara rug on the floor. The man walking forward to greet them would be ideal for a Rolls Royce ad, Whitney decided as her glance flickered over him. Everything, from his artfully styled graying hair to his cashmere sports jacket, was quietly expensive. But there was more to him than his Savile Row tailoring. Whitney was certain a shrewd mind lay behind all his polished perfection.

After they'd exchanged introductions, Morgan Stanringham commented, "I might as well be honest with you, Miss Wakefield. I am opposed to the idea of hiring a contract programmer. I don't like strangers having access to information about my store. Only your employer's impeccable reputation for security convinced me to go along with Bradford on this."

"Mr. Stanringham, I understand your concern," Whitney reassured him. "All the details of your business will stay absolutely confidential. I guarantee it."

"Good. I'm glad we understand each other." He smiled. It was a smile that didn't reach his eyes.

"Now on to the second problem," he continued. "This is the worst possible time to be overhauling our computer system. Our seventy-fifth anniversary sale is coming up, and there will be a flood of merchandise pouring into the store. Still, Bradford convinced me that we need the work done before the next inventory accounting. That's another decision with which I'm not comfortable, but it's too late now." He shrugged. "It will mean a lot of extra work for you, Miss Whitney, trying to keep track of all the special purchase items and goods coming in on consignment while you rewrite the program. Make sure nothing gets lost in the changeover!"

"Morgan," Bradford interjected, "I've been thinking about this problem, and I think the best way to cut down on the confusion would be for only Whitney and myself to have access to the computer while she's working on the new program. We can lock it in with a code."

"That sounds like a logical way to proceed. I'll let you handle all of those details, Bradford. I want to know what code you're going to use, but that's all. The only thing I know about computers is how to read the open-to-buy on the printout they hand me each week."

He stood up to end the interview. As they started for the door, he ordered in a kinder tone, "There is one more thing, Bradford. Please arrange for Miss Wakefield to have our standard twenty-five percent executive discount on anything she buys while she's working with us."

"Thank you very much, Mr. Stanringham. Just walking through your store I've already seen a dozen things I covet. That will help me satisfy my champagne tastes."

When the door closed behind them, Bradford chuckled, "So you're an expensive woman! I'll have to remember that."

"You make me sound avaricious. I simply appreciate quality—in both things and people."

He looked down at her. "I hope I'll qualify."

"Well, I don't know. A man of quality always keeps promises . . . and I'm still waiting for that cup of coffee."

"One cup of coffee for the lady coming right up. Afterward we'll go find Charlie and get you a set of keys to the computer room."

The rest of the day spun by in a whirl of activity. Together Bradford and Whitney started working with the computer. The hours were filled with laughter. Whitney had never felt so quickly at ease with any man before. It was almost as if she'd known Bradford forever, instead of only a few hours. She caught his profile out of the corner of her eye and smiled. Maybe her luck was finally turning. All too soon the chimes rang, signaling the closing of the store.

Bradford seemed reluctant to end the day as they walked out to her car. His eyebrows raised when he saw the metallic blue Porsche. "You weren't kidding when you said you had champagne tastes! Obviously I'm in the wrong business. I didn't know computer programmers made enough money to afford one of these beauties! Where'd you get it?" he asked, walking around the car in admiring inspection.

When she didn't immediately answer he traced a fingertip over the signature of the car dealer. "San Francisco? If you bought this used, you found a real treasure."

She shook her head. "No, I lived in San Francisco before moving here."

Bradford looked at her. A frown creased his forehead. He hadn't missed the slight evasiveness in her answer, but he didn't press the point. He opened the car door on the driver's side for her to slide in. After he slammed it closed he leaned his arms on the window frame. "Whitney, you intrigue me. You're a strong woman, obviously an achiever. That always appeals to me."

Then, as if he couldn't help himself, his fingertips moved lightly in a sensuous caress across her cheekbones, then up to stroke under the smoky darkness of her eyes. "Yet there's a touch of wariness in these brown eyes of yours. It's a fascinating combination."

His touch had such power to disturb her, Whitney had trouble forcing out an answer. "As long as we're confessing, I guess I'd better tell you I've always had a weakness for blonds. They're always—"

The words strangled in her throat. Suddenly she realized how regrettably true her words really were. She drew away from his touch. If anything, she should be repelled by the broad-shouldered Nordic types! After all, hadn't Douglas been blond?

"There you go, retreating again into that private world of yours," Bradford joked, trying to coax the smile back to her lips. "My first instincts were correct. The next several weeks are going to be very interesting!"

Chapter Two

THE STARS were shining brightly that evening when Whitney walked out on her apartment balcony. A warm autumn breeze ruffled her dark hair. As she looked up at the full golden moon, a familiar sadness tugged at her heart. The memory of another harvest moon, that one hanging over the Golden Gate Bridge, returned to haunt her. Would she ever be able to forget that night?

Usually she tried not to think about the past, but tonight all the bitter memories returned. Whitney's hand clenched around the wrought iron railing. Mr. Cramer had shattered with one blow the career she'd struggled so hard to build. That day she'd run blindly out of the brokerage firm and jumped into the blue Porsche; the Porsche that had been her engagement present from Douglas. More than anything she had desperately needed to feel his arms around her. Her foot had pushed the accelerator down farther as she had sped toward his Nob Hill apartment. The moon seemed to mock her unhappiness with its radiant light.

Douglas had held her in his arms while she sobbed out the story, then there was silence. No words of comfort, no words of support. Even with his arms about her she could feel him drawing away. Trembling, she'd pushed out of his arms, then listened while what was left of her world crumbled. Little emotion had shaded his voice as he'd calmly explained why a rising banker couldn't afford to have a suspected thief as a wife. He knew she was innocent, he'd claimed, but he thought they'd better wait until the real thief was caught before setting their wedding date.

Tears now came to her eyes as the rest of the scene

replayed in her mind. With effort she blinked them back.
Douglas hadn't mentioned that his family, the very proper
and very wealthy Johnstons of San Francisco, wouldn't approve
of her in any case, but she'd known the truth. Her
look of disillusionment had finally brought his explanation
to a stuttering halt. As they stood staring at each
other, Whitney had clenched her hand and felt the Porsche
keys cutting into her flesh. It had been an appropriate gift,
hard metal to match his hard heart! Without a word, she'd
dropped the keys on the brass coffee table and turned to
walk out of his life. Only then had a flicker of guilt crossed
Douglas's face as he insisted she keep the car. She had finally
agreed; not because she wanted a memento of their
engagement, but because she knew every time she drove
it, it would remind her what a fool she'd been to love someone
like Douglas! She wasn't going to give her love so easily
again.

Slowly, without really being conscious of it, her thoughts
turned to Bradford. The tears dried as her smile returned.
She walked into her apartment to make a cup of jasmine
tea, then went back outside. As her gaze settled on the
brilliantly lighted Gateway arch towering over the St.
Louis skyline the thought came again: maybe at twenty-eight,
luck was finally running her way. It was a new city,
a new career, a challenging assignment . . . and she'd met
Bradford. The tea warmed her as she took a sip. Or was it
the memory of Bradford's smile, his touch, those unusual
green eyes of his, that was warming her blood? Whitney
stretched lazily, then froze when she realized the direction
of her thoughts. Better stop dreaming! It was always a bad
idea to mix business and pleasure. Besides, for all she
knew he had a wife and seven kids!

Yet as she turned to go inside the memory of his smile
and the way his unusual gray-green eyes seemed to possess
the power to reach in and touch her soul refused to
be banished from her mind. For the first time in a long
time, she sensed that no bad dreams would disturb her
sleep.

The exhilaration of starting a new job jolted her awake
an hour before her alarm was set to ring. After fixing a cup
of coffee she pulled the inventory printout from her briefcase
and started jotting down notes. The ideas came faster

and faster as she began to see how she could restructure the system to run more efficiently. When she glanced up it was after ten.

"Oh, damn!" she muttered, jumping up. "Great way to start! First day on the job, and I'm going to be late!"

To her frustration, even after she arrived at the store she had trouble getting to her office. Shoppers watching a demonstration billed "How to accessorize your wardrobe with scarves" clogged the ground floor aisles. On the way up the escalator she looked back at the milling throng and uttered a silent prayer of thanks that the computer room was tucked quietly behind the crystal and china department, away from all the pandemonium.

The welcome fragrance of coffee greeted Whitney when she unlocked the door. Beside the pot of fresh-perked coffee were set a cream pitcher and two mugs. There was a note propped up in front of the tray that read, "Call me when you get in." It was signed, "Your man of quality." Whitney chuckled as she reached for the phone.

She'd just finished filling the coffee mugs when Bradford knocked on the door. She greeted him with a radiant smile and steaming mug, then nodded toward the coffee pot. "I thought maybe this was your clever way of squeezing more work out of me by eliminating coffee breaks." Appreciatively she took in the crisp scent of his morning aftershave. She couldn't help noticing how his powerful shoulders filled out his flawlessly tailored suit.

"Unjust!" He protested with a laugh.

"Sorry I'm late. I was so anxious to get started on the program that I began working at home as soon as I got up. The time just got away from me."

"You don't have to punch a time clock, Whitney." Bradford grinned at her over the rim of his mug. "That's one of the perks of being an executive. What part of the program did you decide to tackle first?"

"All of the subroutines will have to be rewritten, of course, but the first thing I want to do is figure out a way to link the terminal in the warehouse directly into the main computer here. While I was going over the printouts I noticed there's a lag between the time the merchandise is checked in and when it shows up on the status report. In fact, in a few cases it looks like merchandise might have arrived on the floor and been sold before it got punched into the computer inventory record."

"A bookkeeping crack like that could account for a lot of the shrinkage problems we've been having lately." Bradford smiled. "I knew I was right giving you the contract."

The respect she read in his eyes pleased her. It also gave her a much-needed boost of confidence. "Thanks for the compliment. It always feels good to find that first program flaw, and it will give me something to report when I talk with Mr. Greenwald on Friday."

"Will he be in every Friday for an inspection?"

"No, I report to him once a week at the Your Program Place offices. Other than that I'll be working completely alone."

"Oh, you will?" Bradford asked, his voice softening. "How disappointing. I thought it would be my pleasure to help you."

His accent on the word *pleasure* had been like a caress. It surprised her that just a word could do such unexpected things to her heartbeat. She felt irresistibly drawn to him, and knew the wonderfully strange chemistry touched him, too. She knew nothing about the man, but he wouldn't stay out of her thoughts—and she was glad.

Yet even as she inwardly admitted that, she felt herself pulling away from him. The pain of Douglas's betrayal had scarred her deeply. Would Bradford look at her with such interest if he knew about what had happened in San Francisco? Her mind told her she should tell him about her past, so there would be no secrets between them, but her heart hesitated to take the risk. She turned away to refill their mugs . . . and said nothing.

Bradford took a sip of the hot coffee before smoothly resuming their discussion. "I think we should spend today talking with each of the buyers. They all have complaints about the present system. Also, some departments have unique problems that need to be addressed in your new program."

"That sounds like an excellent idea. Which buyer do you think we should talk with first?"

The shrill ring of the telephone interrupted them, and Bradford answered it. Whitney could hear agitated squawk-

Love's Suspect

ings coming through the receiver. "All right, Millicent, calm down. She's here with me. We'll be right there."

He hung up. "That was the fur buyer, Millicent Hopper. There's a problem in her department we need to check on. From her screeching it sounds like a major catastrophe, but then she always likes to dramatize things."

The carpet in the fur department was littered with price tickets. "Look what the little monster did!" she exclaimed the moment they arrived. "I was in the stockroom for only a moment, and when I came back I found a pint-sized demon yanking off all the price tags. Now how in the world am I ever going to figure out which ticket goes on which coat? I might put a $2500 price tag on a rabbit coat," she fussed, running wild fingers through her already frazzled brown hair.

"Now, Millicent," Bradford soothed, "I know you better than that. You aren't going to make that kind of mistake. But I agree with you, this is going to be a mess to straighten out."

Whitney picked up one of the tickets. It was in four sections and perforated with holes so the computer could read it. "What do these numbers mean?"

Millicent's scarlet fingernail jabbed at the different sets of numbers as she explained. "It gives you the style number, the vendor, and date the merchandise arrived. It's all useless! I've been complaining about those ridiculous tickets for years. Numbers never stick in my brain. I remember furs."

"It's not useless information, and you know it," Bradford pointed out.

"Well then, the tickets don't have enough information on them!" Millicent insisted, refusing to lose the argument.

As Bradford helped Millicent pick up the tickets, Whitney wandered around looking at the magnificent collection of furs. There was every type of coat and jacket available, and even an ermine throw draped across the back of a sofa. She walked across the department to rejoin them.

"I think we can solve your problem, Millicent, by adding one more set of numbers to your tickets. Would it help if I could work out a way to code the type of fur, the kind of garment—coat, jacket, hat, etc.—and the color as well?"

Millicent brightened. "With that information I could have had everything matched up in thirty minutes. But with these tickets it will take days to sort through all the invoices trying to match style numbers and vendors!"

"I'll send someone to help you," Bradford soothed. "I promise you'll have all the information on the new computer system."

"I'd better! Will I have it before the consignment of Raphael Designs furs comes in for the anniversary sale?"

"We'll try. While I'm here, there's something else I need to mention. Millicent, you can't order display racks and have them shipped into the store C.O.D."

"Why not? I wanted them!"

"I didn't say you couldn't have them. It's shipping we're talking about. Let me explain."

As they argued back and forth, Whitney wandered off again. There was a full-length red fox coat hanging on a brass rod. She lifted it down and slipped into it.

Someone behind her let out a low wolf whistle. "Man oh man, that's what I call a really foxy lady!"

She turned around and found a younger version of Charlie, complete with carrot-red hair and freckles, leaning against the rolling rack he'd been pushing. Whitney guessed he was around twenty-two or three. He gave her a big grin as he stuck out a hand. "Hi, I'm Eddie Whitehouse. My uncle said you were a stunner and he wasn't kidding! You have any plans for tonight?"

"Well, you're certainly direct," Whitney commented after shaking his hand.

"You learn to be, in the navy. Sometimes you're only in port a few hours. Got to make the best of what time you have, if you know what I mean." He winked.

"Did you just get out?"

"I sure did. But I've got enough of my land legs back to do some fancy stomping. Come with me tonight to Red Dog Saloon and I'll prove it."

"Sorry, I'm not up on all the latest Western steps."

"Doesn't matter. I'd love to teach you. Just throw on a pair of jeans and come on," he urged with an eager grin.

Love's Suspect   27

"Sorry, Eddie, I can't. I have a pile of computer printouts to go through tonight."

"Well that sure throws salt in my beer. But don't worry, we sailors never give up," he promised, heading off again and giving her a wave good-bye.

Suddenly Whitney felt hands caressing up and down her arms. "I see you met the other half of Stanringham's Don Juan team. Charlie's his uncle."

"So he told me."

"Was Eddie making a pass? I heard his whistle."

"Are you jealous?" she asked, twisting around in his arms.

"Maybe," Bradford hedged. "What did he want?"

"He wanted to take me stomping, that's all."

"Are you going?"

"You know I'm not. Eddie's just a baby." Huskily she added, "I like men."

"And I like women." He leaned toward her and murmured in her ear. "Isn't that a nice arrangement?"

"I can't think of a better one, even though I won't get to learn the Cotton-eye Joe."

"Who says I can't teach you? In fact, there's a lot of things I'd like to teach you, Whitney. Some of them we could even do with the lights on."

"Bradford! You promised."

"I know, but I can't help it. I love it when you blush," he chuckled mischievously as his hands continued their sensuous motion up and down her arms. "I think you'd better take off this coat. I'm beginning to like how it feels on you, and I can't afford to buy it for you any more than you can. I guess we both have expensive tastes."

"Did you get Millicent settled down?" she asked as he helped her hang the fox coat back on the rack.

"It was really your suggestions that did the trick. For someone who's never worked in a retail store you've got some excellent ideas. Let's see if you can do it again. Mr. Agajanian, the Oriental rug buyer, has a different problem. He wants his tickets coded to differentiate between antique and modern rugs, and also a way to tell which carpets are hand tied and which are machine-made."

"Writing this program is getting more complicated by the moment!"

"That's all right with me. The harder it is, the longer you'll be here."

It took the rest of the day to talk with all the buyers. Whitney and Bradford finally started back to the computer room just before closing.

"I'll start working on the computer tomorrow. Since only the two of us will have access to the new program, the first thing I'll need to do is lock it in with a code. Do you have any ideas what we should use?"

"Let's keep it simple. What's your birthday?"

"March seventeenth."

"Ah, you're a Saint Patrick's Day baby. We'll use three seventeen. That should be easy for both of us to remember," he decided.

The computer room door closed behind them, shutting them away from the rest of the store, weaving an irresistible spell of intimacy about them. Whitney felt her breathing surge when she saw desire ignite a spark in his eyes. A husky rasp deepened Bradford's voice as he murmured, "Whitney, I don't want this day to end. Come out to dinner with me tonight."

He moved toward her, but she backed away, shaking her head. "We're moving too fast, Bradford. I don't know anything about you."

"What's there to know? I'm thirty-two, divorced, no kids, and spend more money than I probably should, but I still have enough left to take you out to dinner." His hands, reaching out to touch her, sent delicious waves of sensation scampering up her arms. "Say yes," he urged.

Whitney felt pulled toward a dangerous reef; a reef that could smash the protective shell she'd so carefully erected about her emotions. He stirred desires that were proving hard to resist. Desperately trying to hang onto her resolve she shook her head again. "I don't think it's a good idea to get involved with the boss."

"I agree. I don't like the idea of your kissing Mr. Greenwald at all!"

"That's not what I mean and you know it!"

Bradford released his grip on her arms and took a step backward. "Look, Whitney, I'm not into sexual harrassment. If you tell me to get out of here and never come back

Love's Suspect 29

it can't affect your contract. That's between you, Your Program Place, and Stanringham's. But that's not really the trouble, is it?" he demanded. His gaze probed into the dark depths of her eyes, reading more than she wanted him to see.

A lie hovered on her lips, but when they parted the truth slipped out. "I don't want to go out to dinner with you. I'm afraid I know how the evening will end."

"Would it be so bad to end the evening in my arms? I've never seen more expressive eyes than yours. They can't lie. You're feeling this attraction as deeply as I am."

"I can't deny that, but I'm just not ready to fall into your bed, Bradford. I hardly know you."

"You're right. I don't know you, either. Yet in a way, I feel as if you've been part of my life forever. Maybe it just seems that way because I've been waiting for you forever." His fingers traced over the satiny curve of her cheeks. "Forever is a long time, Whitney, and patience isn't my long suit. You shouldn't blame me for rushing. Right now I want you in my arms so badly I ache."

"But—"

"Did a man put that haunted look in your eyes?" he interrupted. "Is he standing between us?"

"There's no man in my life now, if that's what you mean. But I won't lie to you. There was someone I thought I loved. When he betrayed me, it was shattering. I don't want to make another mistake. It hurts too much."

"I can understand that," he said quietly. "When my marriage fell apart it took me a long time to trust women again."

The silence stretched between them. Finally he spoke. "I know I'm going to hate myself for saying this, but if I promise the evening will end with only a handshake will you have dinner with me?"

Logic warned her to go slowly, but her heart didn't want the day to end either. Emotion won. "How can I refuse such a gallant offer?"

"Gallant or stupid, I'm not sure which. My inclination is to believe the second. Let's go before I come to my senses and withdraw that idiotic promise."

As they walked out of the store into the evening light he

asked, "Shall it be fresh seafood, or would you prefer Italian tonight?"

"I can't resist Italian food."

"Why does your weakness have to be food? Why couldn't it be me?" he protested. "Oh, well, since apparently the only sinful thing on the docket tonight is eating we might as well sin richly. Mario's it is."

The small Italian restaurant was romantically dark with most of the light coming from candles burning in straw-covered Chianti bottles. He handed her a crisp bread stick. "The linguini with clam sauce is wonderful here. If you want something a little less spicy you could order fettucini Alfredo."

"Oh, I definitely like spice in my life!"

"That's not what you said an hour ago."

She brandished her bread stick at him. "One more statement like that, and you won't even get a handshake tonight!"

"All right, I'll quit teasing. But Whitney, I'm not going to quit on this relationship." His hand reached across the red-checkered tablecloth to cover hers. "I'm willing to wait until you know it's as right as I do."

His words brought a glow that lasted through the dinner. The only jarring moment came while they were sipping their after-dinner cappuccino. Bradford gazed at her over the rim of his cup. "I'm curious about you. Whatever made you decide to be a computer programmer?"

"What else can a math major from Iowa State do? Both of my parents were teachers, and I knew I didn't want to do that."

"You could have worked in a bank or a brokerage house. Did you ever consider doing that? Handling stocks and bonds sounds a lot more exciting than sitting in front of a machine punching keys all day."

Whitney's heart pounded. Did Bradford suspect something? Was he trying to probe her past? The evening had been so wonderful. Why did he have to ruin it with questions? She looked into his green eyes and found nothing but normal curiosity.

She shrugged, trying to seem casual. "I find programming exciting. It's a real thrill to run your program and have all the pieces click." She carefully redirected the conversation. "Why did you choose retailing? I think being a spy or an international jewel thief sounds a lot more exciting."

He said with mock seriousness, "How do you know I'm *not* an international jewel thief?"

"Stop teasing me! How did you wind up at Stanringham's?"

"Boring story, but if you insist." At her nod he explained, "I grew up on a ranch in Wyoming, herding sheep and chasing coyotes. Believe me, sheep are some of the dumbest creatures God ever put on this earth, so when the university offered a scholarship I jumped at the chance. Six years later I had my M.B.A. degree, a wife, and a job offer from Stanringham's." A flash of pain twisted his mouth. "I've had a lot of success at everything but saving my marriage."

He didn't speak for a long moment, then he reached across the table to enfold her hand in his. "Whitney, the past is gone. Tonight, let's forget it ever existed. I don't want to talk about my wife. I don't want to talk about that guy who hurt you. Okay?"

Whitney didn't need convincing. "Agreed."

The October night was unusually warm. Bradford wrapped an arm around her waist and snuggled her next to him as they walked out of the restaurant and toward his car.

"You fed me an Italian dinner tonight," Whitney said. "How about letting me cook you a Greek dinner this weekend?"

"Unless you want to fly it down to Texas, I'm afraid I'll have to take a rain check. I leave Thursday to shop the apparel market in Dallas."

"When will you be back?" she asked, hoping her disappointment wasn't too obvious.

"Probably not until Monday or Tuesday. Millicent and I are meeting with the president of Raphael Designs to work out the final details for that anniversary sale fur shipment she mentioned. I don't know how long that will take."

"You're going to miss all the fun. Halloween is this Sunday."

"Somehow I don't think I'll miss Halloween this year.

It's always a time of bewitchment, and I'm getting enough of that from you," he murmured as his fingers gently caressed over her waist. "Will you miss me?"

"Sure. If you're gone, who'll fix the coffee?" Before he could answer her teasing she hurried on. "Besides, I doubt if I'll have time to miss you. I've got a lot of work to do. I noticed there was a portable computer and modem in the computer room. May I take it and work at home this weekend?"

"Excellent suggestion! Remind me tomorrow, and I'll give you the telephone code. I like the idea of you chained to the keyboard while I'm not around. It will keep you out of mischief. Just don't tell Eddie you'll be alone, or he'll be camped out on your doorstep. He's obviously got a crush on you—but I can't say I blame him!"

The moment they'd settled into Bradford's car his arm reached for her again. All the way to her apartment his every touch whispered of desire, a desire Whitney was having trouble denying herself. They were silent riding up in the elevator. Her hands trembled as she tried to force the key into her door. Finally it clicked open.

"Bradford, I—"

"Shhh," he laid a finger across her lips, stilling the words. "Don't talk."

Gently he pulled her into his embrace, molding her body firmly to his. It seemed so right to be in his arms, Whitney had no thought of resistance as she looked up at him. When he felt her relax against him, a fire turned the smoky green of his eyes to emerald. Swiftly, as if he feared she'd escape, he began brushing soft kisses across her mouth. They tasted of such longing she couldn't keep her arms from twining around his neck. It was a gentle possession, but the tremors it aroused were sweet.

Her lips trembled under his as she moved her hands down his chest and slid them under his sportcoat to explore the muscled contours of his back. The touch of his kiss teased her, refusing to be tempted when her lips tried to cling to his. Instead he deserted her mouth to trail a path of fire to her ear. One hand swept her dark hair away, baring her neck to his caress. A light nip of the lobe, the velvety rasp of his tongue as he traced the shell, the warm breath caressing the inside as he whispered her name, sent waves of desire throbbing through her.

Instinctively she moved against him, needing to feel the muscular hardness of his body crushed intimately against hers. She felt a shudder jolt through him as she pressed deeper into his embrace. With a moan he pulled away. Her eyes fluttered open to meet his burning gaze.

"I can't resist you, Whitney. I don't even want to try. You intoxicate me. I can't think when you are in my arms; I can only feel."

She whispered, "This is all happening so quickly. It's insane, yet wonderful. I should tell you to stop, but . . ."

"I don't think it would do any good," he whispered back, and his mouth descended again to claim hers.

There was no teasing this time as his tongue flicked her lips, then moved insistently back and forth across her mouth, begging entry. Willingly her lips parted. Her fingers moved up to tangle in the vital thickness of his blond hair, pulling him even closer as they exchanged pleasure for delicious pleasure.

Their eyes were heavy with need when he drew away. He swallowed, obviously struggling for control as he rested his head a moment against her scented hair.

Finally he took a step away from her. "I knew I was a fool to make that promise, but I did say I wouldn't rush you, and I won't. For tonight, Whitney, sleep well . . . alone." Then, as if looking at her would snap his self-control, he turned and walked quickly toward the elevator.

Once in her apartment Whitney leaned back against the door, trying to force her breathing back to a normal rhythm. She was not at all certain she was glad that he had kept his word.

Chapter Three

Whitney felt the tingle of anticipation as she pushed open the heavy brass doors of Stanringham's the next morning. The job she'd been commissioned to do was exciting, but her assignment wasn't putting the blush in her cheeks. Bradford was. Warm memories of the night before, when his gentle understanding had meant so much, hovered around her as she unlocked the computer room.

A pot of fresh-perked coffee greeted her. Beside it waited two mugs and a pitcher of cream. As she hung up her coat she took a deep breath. The smell of the coffee entwined with the remembrance of their first kiss. Even the thought of it made her heart beat faster as she reached for the phone to invite Bradford down for his first cup.

His secretary's voice was crisp. "Yes, Mr. Prescott is in the store, but he's in a meeting. He shouldn't be tied up more than an hour. I'll have him call you."

Whitney pushed aside a shadow of disappointment that she'd have to drink her first cup of coffee alone. She turned on the computer and punched in the code of her birthday to start the new program running. Thirty minutes later a knock on the door brought an eager smile. It faded when she opened the door. Eddie, not Bradford, was standing there.

"I figured you deserved a sweet treat." He grinned, handing her a huge cinnamon roll wrapped in paper. He walked by her into the room, then stopped in front of the computer and looked intently at the screen. "Wow, look at all those numbers. Do you mean you have your new system running already?"

"Nobody can write a program that quickly. The old system will be operating for quite a while yet."

"How long do you think it will take you? I'd like to know how much time I have to convince you to go out stomping with me."

"I don't really know, but it will be several weeks, I'm sure. There are a lot of problems to work out."

"Hey, that's great!" His face turned red. "I mean, it's great that you'll be around for a while, not that you have problems."

"It's all right, Eddie. I knew what you meant."

The phone rang. Whitney picked it up, listened for a moment, then replied, "Yes, I'll tell him. Good-bye, Charlie."

She put the receiver down, then turned to Eddie. "Your uncle says a truck has pulled in, and they need you down on the dock to help unload it. Thank you for the cinnamon roll."

"Is it enough of a bribe to get you to go out with me this weekend?"

"I'm sorry, but I already have plans."

"For both Saturday and Sunday?"

"Yes, I'm afraid I'll be busy all weekend," she insisted, not telling Eddie she didn't have any plans other than working. She softened her refusal with a smile.

"I guess some other lucky girl will get to enjoy my company. But," he grinned, with as wolfish a leer as his freckled face could muster, "I won't ask anyone else until Thursday just in case you change your mind."

Eddie was gone, but the overpowering odor of his musk cologne lingered. Whitney left the door open. After pouring herself a fresh cup of coffee she sat down at the computer keyboard again.

She was typing rapidly when she heard the door close and felt someone sweep the hair away from her neck. A moment later warm lips traced a kiss across her sensitive nape. "Hmmm that feels good. I didn't know you'd come back . . . Eddie," she teased. "The cinnamon roll was—Ouch!" She yelped as Bradford took a nip at her tender flesh.

His hands descended to her shoulders, and he spun her desk chair around. "Oh, Bradford, I didn't know it was you!" she lied teasingly. "You see, Eddie was here earlier trying to turn my head by bringing sweets."

"I've brought something better than a soggy roll!"

"Oh, and what's that?"

"Myself, and . . . this," he murmured. Strong fingers tilted up her chin a moment before his kiss began to gently brush her lips. Almost instantly their gentle good morning kiss became something else entirely.

Long minutes later, he drew away. She gazed up at him, meeting the fiery green of his eyes.

Bradford reluctantly straightened. "So our cowboy Casanova was pestering you again?"

"I wouldn't call it pestering. He just wanted to know if I was busy this weekend. I told him I was, but he said he isn't giving up. He promised to wait until Thursday to ask anyone else in case I change my mind."

"Do you want me to speak to him?"

"You don't need to say anything, Bradford. I can handle Eddie. He's harmless."

"Okay, whatever you want. I have to admit I agree with his taste in women. The thought of going to Dallas gets less appealing by the minute!"

"Business before pleasure," she chided.

His eyes flashed. "Is that a guarantee there'll be pleasure when I get back?" He bent toward her and searched her eyes.

Whitney trailed her fingertips over the hollowed planes of his face. She added a husky lilt to her voice. "Of course there'll be pleasure when you get back. The pleasure of working out a computer program. The pleasure of organizing the anniversary sale. The pleasure—"

"—of stopping your sassy teasing," he interrupted, his kiss quieting anything else she might say. Momentarily, he drew away. "Unfortunately, I'm on my way home to pack. That's one reason I came down to see you."

"I thought you weren't leaving until Thursday," she commented, trying to hide her disappointment.

"Morgan got a phone call this morning from Raphael Designs. There's some snag with our order for the anniversary sale promotion. I have to fly down early, and either get it straightened out, or find some other company who can ship that many fur coats into Stanringham's." He glanced at his watch. "I didn't even get my cup of coffee, and it's already time to go."

He leaned toward her, but straightened up again. "If I don't hurry I'll miss my plane, yet you're tempting me to linger here! You are a witch—but you're a nice witch. At least I know you'll be home working this Halloween weekend and not out flying around town on your broom."

"If you want me to stay home, you'd better give me that telephone code so I can hook in the modem."

He reeled off a long list of numbers, then reluctantly turned to go. "I'll see you when I get back."

"Do you still think that will be Monday or Tuesday?"

He nodded. "It sounds like a long time!"

With a wave he was gone, and she was again alone. Whitney turned back to the computer. The numbers on the screen were meaningless. She looked around, suddenly realizing how gloomy the room seemed.

With a shake of her head, she tried to clear her thoughts. Bradford wasn't even out of the store, and already she was missing him. That was foolish! She was becoming involved far too quickly, she decided, resting her fingers on the keyboard. Hurriedly she began to type in symbols as if to drown out her heart asking if going slowly was possible— and whether Bradford had touched something too powerful to be denied.

For Whitney the next two days were filled with work, but something was missing. For two years work had been enough; now she was lonely. Each morning the empty coffee pot was a reminder that Bradford was in Dallas.

Late Friday afternoon a phone call summoned her to Morgan Stanringham's office. His glacial smile swept over her like a chill wind as he waved her to a chair. "I know I told Bradford to handle this computer business, but I've changed my mind. I want a detailed report on your progress twice weekly."

Whitney shifted uneasily, suddenly wary. His request didn't bother her—reports were normal operating procedure—but the unwavering intensity of his stare sent a shiver slithering up her back. He seemed to be evaluating her, trying to guess her secrets. Steeling her voice to remain calm, she nodded. "Of course, Mr. Stanringham. You'll have a report on your desk each Wednesday and Friday."

"See that you make it very thorough!"

Love's Suspect 39

She knew his eyes never left her as she walked out of his office. The uneasy feeling stirred by his scrutiny refused to evaporate even after she returned to the solitude of the computer room. When Whitney heard the closing chimes, she gathered up her notes and stuffed them in her briefcase, then placed the phone receiver down in the store's modem so she could work at home over the weekend. With a sigh she loaded her arms with another modem, her coat, and her briefcase, then bent over to pick up the portable computer. It was the size of a typewriter but much heavier. It was quite a balancing act not to drop anything as she struggled toward the escalator.

Eddie came around the corner with an undressed mannequin tucked under one brawny arm. "Hey, you shouldn't be trying to carry all of that stuff!" He patted the mannequin on her bald head. "I've got to drop this ravishing lady off in the display department, then I'll be back to help you. Okay?"

"Really, Eddie, that isn't necessary. I can manage."

"Ah, please! You won't go out stomping with me. At least let me help you tote all that junk to your car."

Nodding her head, she sank down on a sofa in the furniture department. "All right, I'll wait. I can't afford to pay for the damage if I drop this computer."

"Don't let anyone else pick you up. I'll be back as soon as I can."

Five minutes later, Whitney glanced at her watch for the third time. What could be keeping Eddie? After one more minute crawled by she stood up. She was gathering up her things when she saw him loping toward her.

"Looks like you'd about given up on me," Eddie puffed, coming to a stop in front of her. "Sorry it took so long. Miss Hopper grabbed me and wanted me to move some racks of furs for her."

He lifted the computer case out of her hands, then reached for the modem. "What's this black thing? It looks like one of those answering machine gismos."

"No, it's a modem. After I hook it up in my apartment I'll put my phone receiver down into it. It allows this portable computer to communicate over the telephone lines with the main unit in the store."

Eddie glanced out of the corner of his eye at her. "You

said you were going to be too busy this weekend to go out with me, and now you're toting this stuff home. Maybe I could bring over some pizza and beer and—"

Whitney hated to lie, but she really didn't want him hanging around. "I'm afraid that wouldn't work, Eddie," she interrupted. "As I told you before, I have plans. I'm taking the modem home just so it will be there when I do have a few spare minutes."

"Well, you can't fault a guy for trying. Listen, I saw you driving to work in that blue Porsche of yours. You usually park it in the employee parking lot, don't you?"

They met Charlie coming into the store as they were walking out. "Hey, partner, you're going the wrong way, aren't you?"

"I forgot my keys," Charlie explained. He looked at the load Eddie was carrying. "Need some help there, nephew? It doesn't seem fair that you should get all the glory for helping this pretty lady! Why don't you let me carry something?"

"Sorry, but I can manage by myself. I never was one to share glory, especially when I'm trying to impress a foxy lady."

Charlie's only answer was a knowing chuckle as he held open the door so they could walk outside. Whitney's Porsche, parked at the far end of the lot, had a distinct lopsided tilt.

"Oh, great, just what I need! A flat!"

"Hey, don't worry. Where's your spare? I'll change the tire for you."

"Thanks for offering to help, Eddie, but I'm afraid you can't do that. This is the second flat I've had this week. Someone must be scattering nails in the parking lot. The spare's at the garage having a hole patched."

"That's bad luck for you, but good luck for me. Now I get to drive you home. Come on, my Trans Am's over there."

Eddie placed the computer case and modem in the trunk, then unlocked the door so she could slide into the black leather bucket seat. From the way he had touched the sleek curve of the hood as he walked around to his side, Whitney knew how proud he was of his car. As they pulled out of the parking lot, she complimented, "This is quite a car."

"I saved all the time I was in the navy. She was the first thing I bought once I got out."

"Did you get any special training in the service?"

"This will probably ruin my macho image, but I might as well tell the truth. I tried to learn about computers, but I wasn't bright enough. Or maybe," he confessed with a sheepish grin, "I was too busy having fun to study as much as I should have. Anyway, they kicked me out of the program, and I was back swabbing the deck. About all I remember is you have to talk to computers in a special language. Are you using FORTRAN?"

"Yes, that's what the existing program was written in, so I'm staying with it. But enough about my work. Tell me about the navy. I've always thought that must be exciting. Did you sail all the seven seas?"

"You've seen too many recruiting posters. I was in the navy for four years, and except for one cruise to Hawaii and a quick trip down to Acapulco, my ship spent all of its time patrolling the waters near San Francisco Bay. San Francisco's nice, but even it got boring after four years."

"I never got tired of living there," Whitney admitted without thinking.

Eddie's pale blue eyes narrowed. "Don't tell me you were living in San Francisco while I was stationed there."

Her fingers knotted until her nails dug into the palms of her hands. Why had she mentioned San Francisco? She wanted to forget that part of her life! And she certainly didn't want to give anyone clues that might lead to her connection with the bond robbery. Nervously she changed the subject. "I moved away from San Francisco quite a while ago. Did you find someone to go stomping with you this weekend?"

"Sure did. That cute redhead in cosmetics couldn't resist my charm. But I'm willing to dump her if you've changed your mind."

Whitney laughed. "I'd hate to be responsible for this poor redhead's broken heart if you canceled."

Before he could answer she instructed, "Turn right at the next corner, then take a left into the apartment complex. My apartment is in the nearest building."

"Wow, these are pretty snazzy!" As he parked, Eddie

glanced over the mansard roofs and the ornate wrought iron grilles decorating the balconies.

Whitney opened the car door and reached for her briefcase. "Since you're trying to impress me, how about carrying the modem and computer case up to my apartment?"

Eddie whistled cheerfully as they walked into the building, but stopped abruptly when they reached her front door. "I suppose those are part of the country French decor," he observed, pointing to the door's glass panes. "Where's your dead bolt lock?"

"I don't have one. Why?"

"You need one. This door is an invitation to a robber. All he would have to do is break a pane of glass, reach in, turn this knob, and he'd be inside. I don't like you living where it's not safe! Let me get a dead bolt lock and install it for you next week, okay?"

"Yes, Eddie, I'd appreciate that. I never thought about the door, but you're right, it isn't safe. I'll tell the manager you'll be coming so she can let you in. Let me know how much the lock costs, and I'll pay you back."

"We can talk about payment later." He winked at her as he set the equipment on her coffee table. "Now tell me which garage has your spare tire so I can go pick it up and get your car fixed. I'll even deliver it, if you'll give me your keys."

"You don't need to do that. I can call the motor club and have someone take care of it. You've done enough."

"Hey, have a heart, Whitney. I'm not being completely unselfish. I've always wanted to drive a Porsche. This is my chance. Heck, I'd change a dozen tires to get behind the wheel of one of those machines!"

She laughed at his enthusiasm. "Okay, it's a deal." She unsnapped the car keys from her key case and handed them to him. "The tire's at Sam's garage two blocks from Stanringham's."

"I know where that is. But I'll have to wait until Charlie can follow me in my car before I deliver yours. Will tomorrow be all right?"

"Of course. I won't be needing it before then."

Whitney walked with him to the door. "Have fun with your redhead. I'm sure she'll be a much better stomping partner than I would be."

"No way!" He winked again.

After Eddie was gone, Whitney made a pot of tea, then searched in her refrigerator for something to eat. She made a cheese and spinach omelette, then let it get cold as her thoughts wandered to Bradford. What was he doing for dinner? Had he called room service or was he out at a fancy restaurant? She didn't want to think about it, but the inevitable question poked at her anyway. Was he with another woman? The idea of Bradford sharing a glass of Chianti with anyone else hurt.

With deliberate motions she returned the omelette to the skillet and reheated it. After she sat back down at the table she kept her mind firmly fixed on the program she was writing. Still, as she hooked up the modem, she couldn't help wishing that Tuesday didn't seem like such a long time away.

Whitney worked for several hours Friday night and most of Saturday. Her only interruption came Saturday at about six o'clock in the evening when Eddie returned her Porsche and dropped off the keys. He couldn't resist making one more attempt to convince her to go out with him, but he took her rejection with his usual cheerful grin.

After sleeping late Sunday morning Whitney dashed to the store to buy Halloween candy for the trick-or-treaters. Driving home she remembered Bradford's statement about her bewitching him. She hoped she had because he certainly held a powerful fascination for *her*.

Once back in her apartment she dumped the candy bars in a bowl, put it by the door, then sat down again at the computer keyboard and starting typing. It was midafternoon when the trouble started. Suddenly the flow of data slowed down. She jiggled the phone receiver in the modem, thinking it might not be making a good connection, but it didn't help. The computer in the store simply refused to accept her input at normal speed. After struggling with the system for a couple of hours, she switched off the machine.

She scowled as she stared at the blank screen. It didn't make sense. She'd never had a problem like this before, and it confused her. What could be slowing down the data flow? Something was obviously wrong. It could be a problem with her modem connection, or maybe the telephone lines carrying the information were overcrowded. Power surges could be interfering. There could be a dozen explanations.

It was no use wondering about it. Computers were notoriously temperamental. Maybe it had simply decided it had worked enough for one weekend. With a shrug she stood up and dismissed the problem from her mind, realizing it had gotten late. It was probably just as well the computer had gone down. The little gremlins, ghosts, and gypsies would be coming soon, and she hadn't eaten dinner.

The stream of Halloween visitors slowed after eight o'clock. Whitney picked up a book, curled up on the sofa, and unwrapped one of the chocolate bars. An hour later the doorbell rang. One more trick-or-treater must be out making the candy rounds. She picked up the bowl.

Her eyes widened with surprise when she opened the door and saw a pirate, complete with a black eye patch and a shirt slashed to the waist. But there was no mistaking the thick blond hair and broad chest of Bradford Prescott.

"What are you doing here? I thought you weren't getting back from Dallas until next week!"

"You wouldn't want me to miss spending Halloween with my favorite witch, would you? It's trick-or-treat time, my pretty wench."

Whitney's smile turned sultry as she held out the bowl to him. "You're in luck, Sir Pirate. There's booty left for you to plunder."

The pirate glanced down at the candy bars, then took the bowl out of her hands and set it on the table. "That's not the treasure I'm seeking." Bradford's voice was husky with longing as he gathered her into his arms. "I'm after something a lot sweeter than candy."

Chapter Four

THE TOUCH of Bradford's kiss, at first gentle, then deepening with possession, awakened a stirring within Whitney that thrilled and frightened her. For a moment she tried to pull back. Her heart, remembering the pain of Douglas's betrayal, warned her to go slowly. Yet when Bradford's lips moved over hers with coaxing strokes the past lost all meaning. His allure was irresistible, and with a sigh she wound her arms around his powerful neck to pull him even nearer.

Bradford answered her surrender with a throaty chuckle worthy of the most swaggering pirate. Then they were both lost in sweet ravishment as their kiss spun on and on. After long moments he deserted his enticing explorations to move his lips in nibbling circles around the edges of her mouth. In the corner he found a telltale trace of sweetness. He pulled away and, smiling, gazed down into her brown eyes.

"You taste of chocolate. I don't think the trick-or-treaters were the only ones dipping into the candy bowl." His hands tightened about her waist. "I never could resist chocolate."

"Chocolate! Some pirate you make. I expected a much more romantic line from a swashbuckler. Haven't you watched any Errol Flynn movies on the late show?"

He struck a dramatic pose with his feet wide apart and his hands on his hips. As he moved, his shirt opened farther. A flame seemed to scorch through Whitney's fingertips, urging them to reach out and stroke through the mat of blond hair curling across his chest. It took effort to draw her eyes away and listen to his speech.

"You tempt the buccaneer in me, to say nothing of the ham actor. Humor me, my sweet. I've been away at sea for a goodly six months—at least, that's what it seemed like while I was marooned without you in Dallas."

Before Whitney could resist he swept her boldly up into his arms and strode across the room toward the sofa, then sank down on it with Whitney still held warmly in his arms. After settling her in his embrace, his kiss moved down the thread of pulse throbbing in her throat. "Your skin is scented with the spices of the islands," he murmured, staying in character as the first button of her red silk blouse came undone. The second followed as his lips savored the creamy texture of her skin. "It reminds me of the nights we chased the cursed Spanish galleons across the Caribbean. I need a wench to warm me tonight, and you'll do very nicely!"

"I think I ought to take offense at that, Sir Pirate," Whitney teased back, ruffling his hair. "You mean any warm body in your arms tonight would do? I fancy myself to be special."

His arms tightened around her as his body tensed. It was as if her words had hit him like a physical blow. Surprised, she looked up at him and saw a deep frown on his face. He closed his eyes and leaned back his head, almost as if he were angry.

"Bradford, what's wrong? What did I say?"

She felt the tension ebb slowly out of his body. She smoothed a shock of wheat-colored hair back from his forehead. "Bradford, are you all right? Say something!"

When he opened his eyes the mischievous glint was gone. "I could use a drink after the wild time I had in Texas. Shall we go down to Laclede's Landing? I hear they've opened several new spots along the river."

His tone was conversational but cool as he lifted her from his lap and stood up. What had happened? It was as if he had slammed a door shut, dividing them. Why had he drawn away from her? Her lips parted with the question, but the tight set to his shoulders told her it would be useless to ask. She couldn't force him to tell her what was bothering him. She would just have to wait until he was ready.

She fixed a bright smile on her lips. "I'm not sure you

should go down to the waterfront in that outfit. You might get shanghaied."

He shrugged. "Remember, it's Halloween. Besides, I have a coat in the car. No one will even give me a second glance."

Bradford was wrong. Even with his jacket covering the provocative plunge of his shirt more than one woman flicked an appreciative glance over him as they walked along the cobblestone streets of the renovated Laclede's Landing. After one particularly blatant wink of invitation by a passing reveler dressed as a Las Vegas showgirl, Whitney squeezed his arm. "It seems a lot of women want a handsome pirate for Halloween."

"Hmmm? What did you say?"

"Is my company that boring? Maybe I should have dressed up like Salome. That might have kept your attention!"

That finally penetrated the curtain he'd lowered between them. Bradford stopped walking and turned toward her. The light from the wrought iron lamppost at his side ignited the hazel flecks in his eyes. "I admit that would keep my attention. In fact, if you were dressed in the seven veils you'd have gotten so much attention we'd never have left your apartment."

His eyes slowly raked over her scarlet silk blouse, along the curving line of her black linen slacks, then up again. "Yes, you as Salome would be interesting! Shall we try it? Of course, pirates are the jealous type," he said with a roguish tilt to his eyebrows. "I insist you only dance for me."

Whitney's eyes narrowed for a moment as she studied him. Bradford was back to his usual playful bantering as if nothing had happened, and that confused her. He almost acted like *she* had been the one to stop their kisses by suggesting they go for a drink. Why was his mood swinging this evening like a pendulum out of whack?

She sighed silently. Maybe it was just as well. She'd vowed to go slowly. Yet when he touched her, her resolutions dissolved like sugar melting in a gentle rain.

"Well, how about it?" he repeated when she remained silent. "I've got some music from *Scheherazade*. Shall we go to my place?"

Pushing her questions and doubts away, Whitney returned his smile. "Sorry, you're out of luck. My Salome only performs for an audience. And I don't mean just an audience of one!" she added quickly when she saw the spark ignite his gaze.

Bradford's hands moved in sensuous motions up and down her arms. His voice was low. "Even without the dance of the veils you're still the most desirable woman I know, Whitney. If I'm not careful I'll be like Salome's victim and lose my head over you."

The way his voice caressed the word *desirable* sent a surge of heat swirling through her. The breeze off the river ruffled his blond hair as they stood looking at each other.

Hesitantly Whitney answered, "The buccaneers carried off quite a few victims too. Maybe we'd both better be careful."

His expression turned bitter. "You can be careful and still end up . . ." The sentence trailed off as the hurt look twisted his lips again. He took her arm, and they started walking again. "Come on, let's go into Paddy O'Shannesey's and get that drink I promised. I want to hear how you're coming on the programming. On Halloween I suppose you should order a Bloody Mary, but tonight I feel more in the mood for Irish Coffee."

"What? No pirate grog?" she teased, trying to bring back his smile. It didn't work. He remained silent.

Once seated in the restaurant, complete with plaid carpeting and stags' heads, Whitney took a sip of the hot coffee he'd ordered. After delicately licking the whipped cream from her upper lip she looked at Bradford. There was a pensive expression on his face as he stared down into his mug.

What in the world was wrong with him? His wild mood shifts were confusing her. It was a side of him she had never seen before, and it made her feel uncertain. Until this evening everything had been going smoothly between them—and now this. Had she done something? Had something happened in Dallas to put the haunted look in his eyes? She longed to ask what, or *who*, had put it there. As she watched the unhappiness dulling the green of Bradford's eyes, emotion choked her throat. It startled her how much she cared. A few days ago she hadn't known him;

now when he was obviously hurting, she hurt too. And there didn't seem to be anything she could do to help him.

Trying to find something that would erase that look she asked, "You never did explain why your trip to Dallas was cut short." She reached out and put her hand over his. "Believe me, I'm not complaining. I was delighted to open my door and find such a handsome pirate outside. What woman wouldn't! Still, I am curious."

Bradford's fingers curled tightly around hers. His smile returned as suddenly as it had vanished. He brought her hand to his lips for a lingering kiss before letting go. "I could say I rushed things through so I could get back to you. But to tell the truth, when I got to Dallas I found out Millicent, as usual, had blown the problem all out of proportion. If she weren't such an exceptionally talented buyer these storms she enjoys stirring up might get her fired."

"What was the storm about this time?"

"Millicent was upset because Raphael Designs claimed they couldn't deliver as many coyote jackets and coats as she wants for the anniversary sale."

As he talked his fingertips made circles as they traced over the back of her hand. Then turning it over he began to stroke lightly across her palm and up over the sensitive flesh on the inside of her wrist. The movements were causing such disturbing flutters in her pulse that Whitney had trouble paying attention as he continued. "Coyote is the fashion fur this year, and naturally the demand has outstripped supply. Millicent wanted me to put the pressure on to get the order increased."

"Were you successful?"

"After some wheeling and dealing I was. We agreed to buy some lynx coats they were overstocked with, and in return we got the coyote ones Millicent insisted she needed."

He shook his head. "Coyote! It's hard to believe. When I was growing up in Wyoming we used to hunt them and turn in their hides for a twenty-five dollar reward. I wish I'd kept those pelts. They'd be worth a hell of a lot more now! Sometimes I think women will wear anything. The next 'in' fur will probably be skunk."

"Skunk! I don't think so. It wouldn't tempt me. You'd end up looking like a zebra."

Whitney's hand closed over his, stilling the caresses. As their fingers entwined she relished the feeling of warmth radiating from his skin to hers. It was a small thing, but it aroused wonderful stirrings within her.

"I'd prefer that fox coat I tried on. Now that I think about it, one of those lynx coats you bought wouldn't be bad either. As long as I'm wishing I might as well wish for both!"

"There you go again with those expensive tastes of yours. Someday they'll get you in trouble, Whitney."

"It's a good thing I'm not a buyer. I probably couldn't resist temptation."

"Few buyers can!" A scalding bitterness charred his words.

Their mugs were still almost full, but Bradford didn't notice as he tossed some money on the table and stood up. "Let's go, Whitney. We need to talk."

The wind whipping off the river chilled her as they walked along Wharf Street away from the crowded Laclede's Landing. She didn't care. All her thoughts, all her feelings, were wrapped up in the brooding man beside her.

A tug's mournful tooting in the distance was the only sound breaking the silence between them. Finally Bradford's steps slowed. His hands were gentle as he reached to draw her into his embrace. There was no passion as he held her tightly against his chest. It was as if he just needed the reassurance that she was there for him. Finally his hands dropped, and he took a step backward.

In the moonlight Whitney saw his throat move in a hard swallow. "I saw Valerie in Dallas."

"Valerie?"

"My ex-wife. She's a buyer for Neiman-Marcus. We ran into each other in one of the showrooms."

Whitney's hands curled into tight fists. Was that why Bradford's mood had been bouncing around like water on a hot skillet? Had he been trying to find a way all evening to tell her he was reconciling with his wife? Was he going to—? The remembrance of his kiss slashed through these torturing questions. No, his touch couldn't lie. In her heart

Love's Suspect 51

she knew he couldn't have kissed her with such passion while planning to say good-bye.

She reached up and traced over the furrows on his forehead until they eased. "Does it still hurt that much to see her?"

"Not in the way you mean. I looked at her and felt nothing, nothing but sadness over what was gone. What hurt was remembering the pain of watching love die . . . of fighting like hell to save a relationship, only to lose."

"I know," she whispered.

As if drawn by a force he couldn't resist he leaned down and kissed her.

After he drew back from the softness of her mouth he searched her brown eyes before continuing. "I guess seeing Valerie again dredged up all my old uncertainties. It made me think about you and where we're heading. Meeting you has churned up emotions I thought were gone forever. Everything is happening too quickly. It feels both wonderful and frightening." He was echoing her own feelings. "I don't know whether to run, or take you into my arms and never let you go."

Whitney understood only too vividly his confusion. What was happening between them seemed impossible. They'd known each other only a short time, yet she knew with every breath she took that love was beginning to weave its magic web about them. What she didn't know was whether it would be a silken embrace or a terrible trap.

Believe me, the confusion is mutual. "I only know one thing for sure, every day you were in Dallas seemed like an eternity." A soft smile touched her lips. "I perked the coffee in the same pot, but it didn't taste as good without you there to share it with me."

Bradford tucked her hand securely in his. They started walking along the river levee again. "It sounds like you missed me as much as I missed you."

Whitney was pleased to see the harsh lines around his mouth had relaxed. "Missed you?" she teased. "Oh, I don't know about that. How could I have time to miss you when your boss is demanding reports, I have scanning problems every time I try to scroll through the program steps I've entered, and on top of that, this afternoon the data flow—"

He held up his hand. "You're going too fast! Let's take one problem at a time. What's this about Morgan?"

"He's changed his mind. He decided he wants a twice-weekly report from me on my progress," she explained, trying to forget the eerie feeling his hard stare had created.

"Hmmm, that's odd. He usually lets me handle . . ." he shrugged. "Well, don't worry about it. He's just concerned about everything that happens in the store. What scanning trouble are you having? Is something wrong with the computer?"

"No, I don't think it's a malfunction. I don't have any trouble entering my program format, but when I try to scroll back to check something the response time is ridiculous. But the weird thing is, it isn't always slow."

Bradford slapped his forehead. "I knew there was something I wanted to tell you. I thought this might be a problem, but I forgot to mention it. All of the store's cash registers are linked to the main computer. As a sale is rung up the salesperson enters the vendor, style, class, etcetera. That sales information receives priority computer time. That's why during peak sale periods your scanning mode is slowed way down."

"But," she concluded, "my entries don't appear affected because my input time is slow compared to the computer reaction." Whitney frowned. "You know, this could be a real problem later on. The more data I enter the longer the scanning is going to take. By the time my reprogramming is nearing completion it will take hours to run through and find a specific entry. And after this afternoon . . ."

"Whoa, that's enough, Whitney. Let's forget about business, at least for tonight. Okay?"

She glanced at him through her sable-dark lashes. Bradford's hand tightened about hers. The fire was back, sparking the green of his eyes.

"I had lots of time to think about you in Dallas. That bed was so big and so cold . . . and so empty. You can't blame me for dreaming about having your enticing body there beside me with nothing but a sliver of Texas air between us."

The tone of his voice and the passion flashing in his eyes were eloquent. Whitney felt a blush heating her face. "I'm glad you were alone," she confessed. "I've only been at

Stanringham's for a few days, but already I've heard stories about those wild buying trips. I was afraid some buyer might have lured you up to her room."

"Nope, I'm afraid not." He grinned that boyish grin that always jumbled her heartbeat. "I must be losing my touch."

"Poor rejected Bradford. I'll have to think of something to make you feel better."

He dropped her hand so he could encircle her slender waist. His embrace pulled her body intimately against his. "I know how you could make me feel wanted."

"Hmmm. I do, too." Her fingers tangled in the thickness of his blond hair. She nestled closer. "I hate for you to be depressed." Her voice dropped to a husky purr. "I know what you can do. Just believe buyers are only interested in business and not flings. Then you won't feel so unloved!"

She had been joking, but the joke misfired. She'd meant to make him laugh. Instead her words brought back the haunted look to Bradford's eyes.

"I can't believe that, Whitney. God how I wish I could! Those flings are what broke up my marriage."

"Bradford, I'm sorry. Every time I open my mouth tonight I say the wrong thing. I didn't mean to drag up old memories. I wanted this night to be special and now I've ruined—"

He placed a stilling finger across her lips. "You haven't ruined anything. You have a right to know about my past."

"No, you don't owe me an explanation," she answered quickly. "Knowing about your past is not my right. *Now* is all that matters to me. The only thing I care about is that Valerie was fool enough to let you go!"

"Whitney, it is important. I want you to understand. I can't make any promises. I don't know what the future holds, but if we have a future together there must be *no* secrets between us."

Bradford's words jabbed like a spear. No secrets! Was he right? Did their future depend on having no secrets between them? Would the truth about her past drive him away, as it had Douglas? That fear, feeling like a hand tightening about her throat, threatened to choke her. She looked up at him and knew he was becoming too precious to risk losing. Her eyes slid away to gaze out over the darkened river. Someday she'd have to tell him about the theft, the accusations, the shadow of guilt still shrouding her—but not now, not yet.

Bradford's hand cupped her chin and pulled her face gently back until she was forced to look at him. "I know why you're so quiet, Whitney. You want me to swear we have a future together . . . that what we felt from the first moment we met is forever. But I can't do that. If words of love are tossed around too easily they lose their meaning, and I don't want that to happen between us."

Her hand closed over his, imprisoning its warmth against her cheek. "Sometimes it helps to talk about the past. My grandmother used to always say, 'old ghosts die quickly if brought into the light.'"

A wisp of a smile touched his mouth. "It's funny you should say that. Valerie was a ghost when I met her." He grinned, obviously relieved to have the tension of the last several moments broken. "But then so was I, so it didn't matter."

"I knew working so hard would catch up with you. You're cracking up."

"No, I'm not, but the audience did," Bradford observed, fully enjoying her confusion.

Whitney frowned, then her smile broke through. "Audiences . . . ghosts . . . I know! You must have been playing in *Blithe Spirit* when you met."

"Sharp deduction, my beautiful lady, but you've got the wrong play. Valerie and I played George and Marion Kirby in *Topper*. We were the hit of our high school drama club. I always did fancy myself as an actor, but retailing pays better."

"High school? That seems like a lifetime ago."

His smile faded. "I know. When you're eighteen, anything seems possible—even getting married when everyone tells you you're too young." He stroked her ebony-dark hair as he told her about the breakup of his marriage. When Morgan had hired him to be Stanringham's accountant, he'd convinced Valerie to enter the executive training program. "When she became a buyer, she seemed happier, more content. It took me a year to find out why."

His hand reached under the heavy sweep of Whitney's

Love's Suspect 55

hair to caress the nape of her neck as if seeking the reassuring warmth of her flesh. She knew he needed to talk out his feelings, so she remained silent as his words tumbled on.

"For Valerie, the buying trips to New York opened her eyes to a new world: a world of glamour, of excitement. We married so young she never experienced all the wild and crazy things teenagers try. Maybe that's why she couldn't resist the temptations so freely available in New York." The motions of his hands ceased. Whitney felt his fingers tense.

"Our marriage had been teetering for months. Looking back I suppose love was already gone, but I just didn't want to admit it. All I know is I couldn't let go without trying to save what we had once had. When Valerie left on another buying trip I thought flying up and surprising her with a visit might help."

His bitter laugh echoed over the water. "Surprise! It sure as hell was that! I'll never forget that night. The bellhop let me into her room. The lights were romantically dim, a champagne bottle was on the table . . . and Valerie was in bed with her lover. I found out later he wasn't the first. After I walked out on her that night she went on a spending spree. When we divorced six months later I ended up with a used dinette set and half the bills. I'm still paying them off."

In that moment Whitney felt closer to Bradford than she ever had to any man before. They'd both experienced the same ache of betrayal. She knew what he was feeling, thinking, needing.

Moving closer, she slid her hands up under the lapels of his jacket. Through the wool she could feel the beat of his heart. It was hypnotic in its power to reach into her mind and make her speak without thinking of the promises she'd made herself or the consequences.

Her brown eyes searched and found the green depths of his. "Bradford, come home with me. We've both been alone too long."

As they looked at each other, desire, enveloping like a velvet cloak, wrapped its warmth around them, protecting them against the chill of the night . . . and the past.

Chapter Five

Whitney reached to turn on the lights in her apartment, but Bradford stopped her. He gently pulled her hand away from the switch. Their fingers twined as if each needed a touch to convince themselves this moment was real.

"The moonlight on the river was part of tonight's magic. I don't want it to end," he murmured as he led her toward the balcony doors and opened them.

"Won't it be a little chilly?"

"Trust me. Together we can light a fire that will keep us both very warm!"

Through the open doors the silvery light spilled across the two of them, creating a mood as romantic as any candlelight. Bradford gazed at Whitney a long moment, then gathered her into his embrace. The touch of his kiss was tentative, searching, waiting to see if she would draw back. Her lips answered, softening under his. Without words they spoke of her need to hold him, to feel close to him, to belong to him totally.

With a contented sigh he pulled just far enough away from the honeyed sweetness of her mouth so he could look down into her face. There was no urgency. They both knew the night held many wonderful hours.

He moved a finger across the skin over her cheekbones. "You have such beautiful eyes. I never knew brown eyes could be so expressive. I almost feel I can read your every thought through them."

"What are they telling you now?" she asked softly.

One corner of his mouth curled up in a grin. "The message couldn't be clearer. And I admit I'm surprised. I never knew women had such ideas! Tonight should be interesting."

"Bradford!" Whitney tried to make her voice stern, but a guilty giggle escaped when she remembered exactly where her thoughts *had* been straying a moment before.

"I love it when you blush. Women who are too blasé to blush bore me."

His hands encircled her waist, but he didn't move to bring her more intimately against him. Instead his fingertips began to take delightful forays along the waistband of her black linen slacks. Expertly he undid one button of her silk blouse, allowing his hand to slip inside to find the warmth underneath.

Every inch of her seemed to come alive as his caress moved across her bare skin, leaving a trail of fire in its wake, stirring her blood.

"Shall I tell you what I really see in those wondrous eyes of yours?" he asked as his touch continued tracing delectable patterns under her blouse. Without waiting for her answer he murmured, "I see caring and trust. I've been waiting a long time to see that."

Whitney found it difficult to breathe as his velvety fingertips moved upward. Her breasts yearned to be possessed by his caress, yet he stopped before reaching them.

"I wanted you the other night. I want you now. I want you desperately, but I'm greedy. I want you to come willingly into my arms with no doubts to hold even a tiny part of you back from belonging completely to me."

"Belonging completely," she repeated. "I guess I've always known that's the only way it can be between us, and it scared me."

"Don't be scared. I know what it is to be hurt. I would never do that to you. But I want more than a casual fling."

A loving smile crossed her lips. "I am yours, Bradford, completely yours."

"Prove it. Prove it now!" he whispered with a compelling urgency that shattered any hesitation, any modesty, she might feel.

She made the first move. His pirate shirt, slashed to the waist, still tempted her. All evening her fingers had burned to explore the blond furred chest she'd glimpsed underneath. Nothing stopped her now as she reached for him. The muscled planes of his chest sent irresistible waves of need tingling through her hands. As they moved, the heat of his skin began sending the message to the rest of her body.

At her caress his eyes fired to a glittering jade, but she didn't back away from sensual demands she saw there. Instead her lips opened in invitation; an invitation he quickly answered. As first their lips, then their tongues, met, his hand finally reached to ease the ache throbbing through her breasts.

Button after button fell open. The scarlet silk of her blouse parted, giving them the intimate contact they both craved. With deliberately arousing strokes Bradford's fingers flicked over the peaks, thrusting against the wispy lace of her bra, then retreated. The lace was like a veil, taunting, teasing, promising how exquisite it would be when nothing separated them. Still he didn't hurry this delicious building of desire as his hands roamed over her back, her waist, before returning to cup the fullness of her breasts.

"Your skin is like fine-spun silk, only more beguiling than that." His voice sounded muffled as he planted a line of kisses down into the warm valley between her breasts. "You even taste good. I don't think I'll ever tire of holding you."

His gaze raised to meet hers as his fingertips trailed a caress across the lush curve left provocatively bare above the lace of her bra.

Whitney answered his caresses with ones of her own, reveling in the muscular hardness of his trim waist, the breadth of his shoulders, the curly hair tickling her palms as she moved her hands across his chest. A throaty richness colored her voice. "Touching you only makes me want more."

When he gathered her back tightly into his embrace both knew the time for words was over. As his touch stamped his ownership on her flesh, the desire within her unfurled like a flower opening to the rays of the sun. Like the sun, the desire first warmed then burned her skin, demanding relief; a relief she knew she could find only in his arms. Driven to feel closer, she moved her body against his in the timeless ritual of need. The surging power of his response thrilled her and left no doubt he was experiencing the same sensual magnetism that was enthralling every nerve within her body.

For a long moment she reveled in the intimate dance their hands, their bodies, their tongues were performing, then drew away. His eyes burned as he gazed down at her. She smiled, knowing the fire was as hot in hers, then took his hand to turn toward the bedroom.

He didn't move. His gentle tug urged her back into his arms. "The moonlight is here, Whitney. Let's enjoy it."

She glanced down at the square of gold carpeting made luminous by the soft moonlight flooding through the balcony doors. "On the floor?" She tried to suppress a smile, but failed. "Isn't that a bit decadent?"

"Sure it is. That's part of the fun!" he chuckled with pretended depravity. "I'm playing a pirate tonight. We buccaneers take our wenches where we find them."

Then he sobered. As his hands gently stripped the blouse from her shoulders then reached to unclasp her bra, he murmured, "Ah, my beautiful Whitney, you make me feel so many things. When I hold you I do feel wickedly decadent. I want to touch, to know every inch of your body. I want to feel you under me and experience the passion of your lovemaking. But I want more than just that. I also want your tenderness, your compassion, your understanding . . . everything that makes you so special."

Bradford unsnapped her slacks. His hands brushed her thighs. She trembled as he drew the black linen down her slender legs. When her slacks were tossed aside he stepped back. His hands fell to his sides.

"It's your turn. Undress me." The words were a command, yet his eyes pleaded. "I want to feel your touch."

She experienced a second of shyness, but the passionate note of longing in his voice overcame the feeling. She moved confidently toward him.

When the only thing between them was a shaft of moonlight, Bradford put his arms about her. Her responding embrace found his waist, and for wondrous moments they stood locked together, savoring the sensuous textures of being man and woman. His hair-roughened body played against the smoothness of hers. He pulled her closer until the curve of her breasts flattened against his broad chest.

Then when his muscular thigh found its way between the softness of hers, the desire flared too hot to resist any longer.

Together they sank down on the floor. Tenderly he laid her back against the carpeting, then rocked back on his heels. His glance swept slowly down over her as if he were storing the memory of how her skin, her eyes, the dark hair spilling out about her, looked in the silvery moonlight. Whitney thrilled to see the passion in his expression as he gazed at her. But seeing wasn't enough. Every part of her yearned to experience the power of that passion.

She smiled, opening her arms wide to welcome him.

He lowered himself into her embrace. When his lips were a breath away from hers he swore, "No more pirates, no Salome, no tricks. All that is left for this Halloween is the treats. I promise they will be sweet."

They were. It was sweeter than anything she'd experienced before. A moment after his kiss possessed her mouth all the desire their caresses had lovingly built ignited into an explosion that sent a shuddering wave through both of them. It was like a forest fire in its power to consume everything but their driving need for each other.

The moonlight, splashing its radiance over them, made the moments even more magical. Under its soft glow they exchanged sensuous pleasure for pleasure. A kiss, a touch, a caress, each pulled them higher until Whitney thought the passion couldn't become any more exquisite. But it could, and it did.

Finally all thought was lost to sensation. Only feeling, experiencing, remained.

"Oh, Bradford! Bradford!" Whitney moaned his name over and over again with a rhythm that echoed the cresting waves of desire firing through them. As he had wanted, she finally belonged completely to him.

Only slowly did they come down from that wondrous pinnacle. They were so warm and comfortable in the embrace that time drifted sweetly away, neither wanting to break the moment by moving. They snuggled, exchanged a loving kiss, not of passion but one of whispered gratitude for the pleasure just exchanged. Then they dozed.

The moon was on its downward journey when Whitney felt strong arms lifting her from the carpet. Her eyelids, the heavy eyelids of a woman well satisfied, fluttered open only to close contentedly when she saw they were heading toward her bedroom. Her arms went around his neck, and she placed a kiss against the tanned column of his throat.

"Rhett Butler, I presume," she murmured, savoring the delicious feeling of being held securely against his chest.

"Of course, Miss Scarlett."

"Being carried to bed in a lover's arms is every woman's fantasy. Too bad we don't have a sweeping staircase to make this perfect."

In the dim light she could see Bradford's smile. "Wait until you come to my apartment, Miss Scarlett. If all the fantasies are fulfilled in one night, it leaves nothing to dream about."

As if the sensation of being near her was too precious to lose, his touch never left her as he folded back the comforter and tucked her into bed. When the warm length of his body slid in next to hers she nestled close and wrapped her arms around him. With the thudding of his heart beating reassuringly in her ear she fell asleep.

For two years, frightening dreams of the glaring lights at police headquarters, uneasy dreams of the unrelenting look in Mr. Cramer's eyes when he'd fired her, sad dreams of Douglas's nervous clearing of his throat but saying nothing as she'd walked out of his life, had been Whitney's constant nighttime companions. Now these dreams lost their power to haunt her. Protected in Bradford's arms, she slept peacefully.

At dawn, pleasant thoughts floated through Whitney's mind. She was in a meadow lying on a bed of soft green grass. A smile touched her lips as she imagined she could smell the heady fragrance of the wild flowers blooming all around her. A warm breeze tickled the backs of her legs, and she stretched, enjoying the feeling. Then softly, like the brush of a butterfly's wings, she felt something nibbling on the back of one knee. Her sleep-drugged mind reeled. Why did the breeze or butterfly wings feel like kisses?

Kisses . . . Bradford . . . last night. She smiled and let the dream escape. With a contented sigh, she murmured, "In my dream I thought you were a warm breeze."

"A warm breeze?" he asked, between the delightful

tasting bites that were slowly edging their way upward. "Some dream! I'd at least like you to think of me as a powerful wind, even a tornado maybe."

"Why? A breeze is better."

His kiss, exploring the inside of her thigh, touched off ripples of sensation that drove away the last mists of sleep. "The touch of a breeze is *much* better!" she repeated, unable to keep the husky tone of rising desire out of her voice.

His knowing chuckle was the only answer as his lips deserted one knee to sample the delights of the other. "Bradford, that tickles!" she protested with a giggle when he hit a sensitive spot.

"Does it? Okay, I'll start taking harder nibbles."

"Don't you dare!" She tried to wiggle free, but he held her easily.

"You can't go anywhere. I haven't finished the ankle inspection," he mumbled, stroking a kiss down her calves. "I never could resist beautiful legs."

Teasingly she pulled her ankle away from his explorations and curled her knees up under her until she was kneeling on the bed facing him.

Bradford, with the grace of a tawny lion, sprang quickly up to confront her. His hands reached out and closed over her bare shoulders. "Do you object to being called a woman who has it all? Intellect to touch my mind, and beauty so enchanting my pulse races just looking at you."

"That sounds like a line our cowboy Don Juan, Eddie, would use," she jested.

His hands tightened on her shoulders. "The truth is never 'a line.' You are everything I've been searching for."

"Bradford, I'm not—"

"Whitney, please let me finish. I want you to understand. I'm not a saint. There have been other women in my life since my breakup with Valerie, but flings only satisfied one part of my need. They left a loneliness I feared might never be cured. I'd almost given up hope of finding someone as perfect as you." A crooked smile turned up one corner of his mouth. "In fact, I'm not sure I deserve you. You're almost too good to be true."

The black specter of the secrets she was shielding from him rose to remind her how far from perfect she really was. Her hands reached out to caress the rugged planes of his face. "I wish you would listen to me. I've never tried to tell you I'm perfect. I'm not. How do you know you may not deserve someone a lot better?"

"That is a point to consider," he grinned, sliding his hands down to her waist. With a quick tug he tumbled her back against the pillows, then followed her down, trapping her seductively into the lush warmth of the bed. "Maybe I'd better make another test just to be sure."

Whitney opened her mouth to protest, but his kiss descended to steal away her words. The theft was too sweet to resist. Her arms wound around his neck to urge him more intimately into her embrace as her lips softened willingly under his.

Her last conscious thought, until all was lost to the sensual rapture their hands and their kisses were creating, was that there was always tomorrow . . . or the next day, to tell him the truth about her past.

Chapter Six

Bradford's hand dropped to the ornate brass handle on one of the doors of Stanringham's, yet he didn't pull it open. His gaze sought Whitney's through the glare of the early morning sun, then his free hand reached to lace its way through her fingers. She saw hesitation in his eyes. They both knew inside the store would be telephone calls, problems, pressures; endless things to keep them apart. The hours he'd held her in his arms the night before, their passion of the dawn, had been so perfect he obviously hated for it to end as much as she did.

From inside the store she heard the chimes ring out the time, nine-forty-five. In fifteen minutes customers would be streaming into the store. They had no choice. It was time to part. She tried to make it easier. "It's lucky you had your luggage in the car. Otherwise you'd still be in your pirate costume. I wish the bewitchment of Halloween could go on forever, but I know it can't. I guess it's back to work." She glanced at the door and let a sigh escape. "Reality returns."

Bradford brought her fingers to his lips for a lingering kiss. His lips caressed each fingertip before he said, "Whitney, what happened last night is as real, as important to me as anything I'll do inside Stanringham's."

"Better not let Mr. Stanringham hear you say that. I get the feeling he doesn't believe anything in the world is as important as this store."

"You're right about that! And if you met his wife you'd understand why he feels that way. Blanche is a beautiful fashion plate, always sponsoring the correct charity ball, but I'm not sure there's anything behind the glittering facade. I'm glad you aren't putting up a facade like that . . ." he hesitated for a second, then added, "Are you?"

She felt emotion tighten her throat and knew anything she said would sound strained. She merely shook her head.

He waited a long moment as if expecting her to say something else. When she didn't, he pulled open the heavy door. As they walked by the fine jewelry counter toward the escalator she slanted a glance up at him. Why did he have to keep saying things that hooked her guilt about the secrets she was shielding from him? Did he suspect something? Or was she imagining undercurrents to his words that weren't there?

Looking at him she wished she knew. There was only one certain thing. She wanted to forget the past, yet it wouldn't go away. Even now it threw a dark shadow between them that shaded the joy she felt being with him. Maybe she should tell him the truth, her mind argued. Her heart feared to take the risk. As usual, emotion won. She said nothing.

Whitney was so lost in thought that she jumped when she heard Morgan's less than friendly greeting. "There you are, Bradford. Where have you been? I called Dallas, and Millicent said you'd left for home. So then I tried your apartment until all hours last night and never could—"

His words halted abruptly as he glanced from Whitney to Bradford, then back again. A speculative look narrowed his eyes, turning them an icy gray-blue.

"Oh."

The intonation of Morgan's voice placed a trainload of meaning on that one simple word. His glance, sweeping down over Whitney's trim navy suit, added a cynical twist to his mouth. There could be no doubt in her mind that Morgan guessed correctly where Bradford had spent the night. She felt a hot blush heat the skin across her cheekbones, but she refused to look away. She might feel guilt over hiding her past from Bradford, but she felt *no* guilt over what had happened the night before.

Bradford's question bridged the awkward moment. "What's the problem, Morgan? It must be a class A crisis if it couldn't wait until this morning."

The older man glanced again at Whitney as if trying to decide whether to discuss the matter in front of her, then shrugged. "It's the truckers. Charlie heard from one of the drivers on the docks that we may have one helluva crisis. The cross-country haulers are threatening to go out on a wildcat strike. If they do we can kiss the anniversary sale good-bye. The sale kicks off next week, and if we don't receive our merchandise we're in trouble. We don't even have enough stock on hand to be able to run the first week's ads on the televisions and video recorders."

"How about having the goods shipped in by rail? It will take longer, but we'll be assured of delivery," Bradford suggested.

"I don't care if we have to air-freight the damned stuff in, just get it done! We've got too much riding on this. Nobody, not the truckers or anyone else, is going to wreck our seventy-fifth anniversary celebration!"

As Morgan issued this last statement his glance swung again to Whitney. When he looked at her every muscle stiffened. The glacial hardness of that stare yanked her back two years when another man had hurled accusations at her. Whitney's breath felt as if it were strangling in her throat. Two years ago it had been the bond theft. But why was Morgan looking at her with that same expression? His eyes accused, but she hadn't done anything wrong. The question pounded again and again through her mind. She had no answer.

The silence seemed to stretch forever. Finally Bradford spoke, and the tense moment ended as Morgan's attention turned away from her. "Don't worry, we'll get the merchandise," Bradford reassured him. "Charlie's news may only be a rumor, but just in case I'll set up alternate shipping plans."

"This is all we need! We already have enough trouble to last a year."

"Morgan, ease off. Even if they do call a wildcat strike, I've seen the projected sale profits. The volume of sales generated should easily offset any added shipping costs."

"I'm not talking about shipping costs! I'm talking about inventory control." His fist clenched, emphasizing the words. "Moving merchandise from trucks to trains and back to trucks means trouble. It's more movement to keep track of, and we have enough trouble with security and inventory shrinkage without that! You know as well as I do that we've lost several entire shipments that way already this year." He flung one more hard glance at Whitney, then stalked off.

When Morgan was out of sight, Whitney turned toward Bradford. A worried frown furrowed her forehead. "I don't think your boss likes me. Care to tell me why? Those looks he threw me would have frozen boiling water."

"Don't worry about it." Bradford gave her a reassuring squeeze on the arm. "It's not *who* you are, it's *what* you are that's the problem."

Whitney cocked her head to one side. "Well, that's certainly a cryptic remark." She indulged in a teasing addition. "What I am is a woman."

"I know!" His voice sounded like the purr of a contented tomcat. "You proved that most convincingly several times last night."

As usual she couldn't help responding to his tone. The scolding on her lips melted into a laugh as the vivid memories of the night before filled her mind. With effort she gathered her delightfully wandering thoughts to order. "Is that the trouble? Does Mr. Stanringham disapprove of our relationship?"

"Hell no, he's probably jealous." Bradford tilted a raking eyebrow. "What man wouldn't be?"

She rewarded his compliment with a smile, but didn't back away from the question. "Then what is it?"

He glanced around. Everyone appeared busy getting ready to open the store, but nevertheless he suggested, "It's never a good idea to discuss the boss's foibles in public. Let's go to your office."

As they rode up the escalator Whitney felt again a stab of apprehension, remembering the accusing expression on Morgan's face. It brought back too many frightening memories. It took effort to keep her hand from trembling as she fixed the coffee.

Bradford seemed to sense her uneasiness because he filled the awkward moments with an amusing story about Millicent's confrontation with the Soviet Embassy over some Russian sables she wanted for the store. By the time the coffee finished perking Whitney believed she was back in control of her emotions enough to finish their conversation.

Love's Suspect   69

She handed him his morning cup of caffeine. "All right, we have privacy now. No one's going to bother us. This computer room is so secluded I sometimes feel as if I'm on a deserted island. So tell me, what's bothering the big boss? When he looked at me a few minutes ago I felt I should dive for the nearest foxhole."

Bradford rubbed the back of his neck as if searching for a place to begin. Finally he said, "You have to understand about Morgan. In a very real way this store is his life. He feels as protective about Stanringham's as a father watching his little girl leave on her first date with some guy who drives a van. It isn't you. It's the fact that you're doing the programming for our new inventory system."

Whitney frowned in confusion. "I'm sorry, I still don't understand. He hired me."

"Remember what he said that first day? He agreed to hire you, but he admitted he still wasn't happy about it. He's a real security nut," Bradford explained. "He hates the thought of an outsider knowing the store's business. And I admit he has good reason. Some of our competitors will go to any length to torpedo Stanringham's success. Earlier this year a copy of our complete inventory accounting disappeared. That book contained our vendor list, markups, markdowns, projected classification changes—in sum, everything about the store's operation. I'm sure it was sold for a very good price. Whoever got their hands on it learned a lot of valuable information. It's easy to see why Morgan gets a bit paranoid once in a while."

"I'm not going to sell Stanringham's secrets to the highest bidder!" she protested.

"I know that, but Morgan doesn't. He doesn't know anything about you, so he's suspicious. You'll have access to a lot of very valuable information. So, I'm afraid he'll be watching you very carefully."

Mistrust, suspicions . . . all the ghosts from her past were rising to haunt her again. The thought of someone watching her brought chills.

"Whitney, what's wrong? Your face went absolutely white. Not hiding the proverbial skeleton in the closet are you?"

"No, of course not!" she answered too quickly.

Immediately she was chiding herself. The words denied,

yet the speed with which she'd whipped out that denial made it sound like the truth was just the opposite.

She saw the doubt, the concern, clouding his eyes and pasted on a smile. "Don't worry, I'd like to claim I was the Mata Hari type, but I can't. The only thing in my closet is the usual accumulation of junk. You might find a deflated beach ball and a faded swimming suit or two, but you won't find a skeleton, I promise. If you're not busy tonight you can come over for a closet inspection."

She forced a laugh. "I was just being foolish. As I told you the day you hired me, succeeding at this job is very important to me. I overreacted, that's all. When you said that about Mr. Stanringham, I had a sudden vision of his distrust building until he canceled my contract. I'd be out before I could prove myself."

To her surprise Bradford curled reassuring fingers around her forearm. "I guess you really should blame me, not Morgan. In a way this mess is my fault. I should have explained about Morgan's hang-ups before you signed the contract, but I didn't want to scare you off." Before she could reply he tried to lighten the mood by joking, "After all, I'm not stupid. The next programmer they sent might have weighed two-fifty and had a wart on her nose. I figured I'd better hang onto what I had." He winked as his hand found the womanly curve of her waist. "And you have to admit, I've been hanging on ever since!"

Whitney tried to respond to his teasing, but he saw her uncertainty. His embrace gently squeezed her as he reassured, "Don't worry, once Morgan realizes you aren't going to steal anything he'll leave you alone."

"I hope so!" The plea came from the deepest part of Whitney's heart. "I am not a thief, Bradford."

"Of course not," he agreed, planting a kiss on the tip of her nose. "But unfortunately, I won't be able to make that closet check. I'll have to spend the morning making contingency plans in case the truckers strike. That means my budget meetings will be delayed until later this afternoon. The way those things drag on we'll probably be up to our elbows in black ink until midnight. Usually I look forward to planning the merchandising budget for the next season, but not today. I think you're a bad influence on me . . . but I'm not complaining!"

Love's Suspect   71

When his hand touched the doorknob, Whitney blew him a kiss. "Think of me," she whispered.

A big smile splashed across Bradford's face. "If I do that I'm liable to allot all the open-to-buy to the sexy negligee department!"

The glow left by Bradford's presence lasted until Whitney turned on the computer and called up the program she was working on. Neat columns of numbers filled the screen, but the only images registering in her mind were the silent accusations she'd seen in Morgan's eyes. Even her feelings for Bradford weren't strong enough to shield her from the fears left by her past. Her fingers, resting on the keys, trembled.

With a muffled oath she shoved her chair back and went to pour herself another cup of coffee. "Who's being paranoid now?" Whitney muttered to herself. "A man looks at you, and you start imagining all sorts of nonsense. If this keeps up you'll soon be ready for a one-way pass to the funny farm."

"I knew I shouldn't have left you alone."

Eddie's voice made her jump. She whirled around to find him leaning against the doorjamb. The freckles wrinkled up across his nose as he grinned. "You see what happens when you spend a weekend alone? You start talking to yourself. When will you learn I'm always right? Solitude is only good for monks. You'd have been a heap better off if you'd come stomping with me."

"And let you disappoint that cut redhead in the cosmetics department? How could I be so cruel?" Then, without thinking, she added, "Besides, I had work to do."

Eddie's eyes widened. "Hey, I thought you said you weren't going to work this weekend! At least, that was the story you handed out when you broke my heart."

His big blue eyes reminded her of a little boy who'd lost his prize marble. "What's the matter?" he asked, looking like a whipped puppy. "Do you have a thing against men with freckles?"

His antics made Whitney chuckle. "Tell me, Eddie, were you born with a line or did you develop such style in the navy?"

"I'll never tell. It's a trade secret." He handed her a paper sack. "I brought this for you. I decided the cinnamon roll I gave you last week was a tactical mistake. You're a classy lady. This time I brought almond croissants!"

She unfolded the top of the bag and glanced in. "There are two croissants here. Is that a not-too-subtle hint you'd like to share them with me?"

"Sure is. You never get to first base with the ladies if you're subtle. I learned that in fifth grade from Emily Lou. But enough about my scandalous past. We have something we need to discuss. Why not combine business with croissants?"

She handed him his roll and asked firmly, "What business?"

The tone of her voice stopped his flirtatious banter. "All right, I'll behave. I really came down here to find out when I can come and change the lock on your door. I've been worrying about it all weekend. Are you going to be home tonight . . . home alone?"

Whitney knew he was fishing, but she refused to take the bait. "As a matter of fact I am going to be home, and I do want that lock changed. If you promise to behave I'll even invite you to dinner. That is, if you don't mind hamburgers. That's all I've got in the freezer."

"Wow—dinner! That's almost better than an evening with you at the Red Dog Saloon."

Whitney shook her head. It was impossible not to like Eddie. He had the enthusiasm of an eager puppy, and while his attention was flattering she didn't want him to get hurt. "Remember, it's just a thank-you dinner, nothing else."

"I know, but I can still hope my engaging charms will win you over eventually." He looked around the computer room while munching on his croissant. "Where's all that stuff I lugged out of here Friday? Did you leave it at home?"

"Yes, but I might as well have brought it back. It didn't work very well."

"Oh?"

"I tried to work Sunday afternoon, but the data input-output slowed down so much it was useless to keep punching in more symbols. Something must have been wrong with the modem or on the telephone line. I finally gave up."

Love's Suspect

Eddie shook a finger at her. "That's what you get for trying to work at home. You might as well have been out having fun with me."

"I'm not sure about that, but I agree working at home isn't the answer. Do you think I could get a key to the store? That way I could come in here whenever I need extra time on the computers."

"Well, I don't know." Eddie scratched his chin. "No one's supposed to be here after hours, but what the heck. Sure. I'll tell Charlie to bring you one. I'd like to help. Besides, according to the Eddie philosophy of courting, it never hurts to have a lady beholden to you. How much time do I have to get my fatal charm working? That is, how soon are you going to have the new system running?"

"Right now I'm working on a looping pattern that will feed inventory information directly from the warehouse into the data base, and that's only the beginning. It's a very complicated program. Unless some miracle happens it will be a couple of weeks."

"Great. Then there's still hope for me!"

Whitney couldn't resist smiling at his unending optimism. "Part of your courting philosophy ought to be learning when to give up."

"Never!"

"Don't blame me, I warned you it's hopeless. But thank you for helping me get a key to the store. I appreciate it."

He stood up and brushed the crumbs off his hands. "Hate to hit the road, but I'm afraid I have to. There's just one thing: take my advice and don't mention this key business to Mr. Prescott or Mr. Stanringham. I don't want any of us to get in trouble. Charlie's too old to be hunting for a new job now."

He turned to go but stopped in the doorway. "Oh, by the way, you'd better call and tell Charlie when you plan to be in the store so he can fix the alarm system. We don't want you busted by the fuzz for breaking and entering, do we?"

"What about the night watchman?"

"No need to have one with our new alarm system. See you tonight. I'll bet those hamburgers of yours will be tastier than a steak broiled over good ol' mesquite wood."

Love's Suspect   73

Eddie shook a finger at her. "That's what you get for trying to work at home. You might as well have been out having fun with me."

"I'm not sure about that, but I agree working at home isn't the answer. Do you think I could get a key to the store? That way I could come in here whenever I need extra time on the computers."

"Well, I don't know." Eddie scratched his chin. "No one's supposed to be here after hours, but what the heck. Sure. I'll tell Charlie to bring you one. I'd like to help. Besides, according to the Eddie philosophy of courting, it never hurts to have a lady beholden to you. How much time do I have to get my fatal charm working? That is, how soon are you going to have the new system running?"

"Right now I'm working on a looping pattern that will feed inventory information directly from the warehouse into the data base, and that's only the beginning. It's a very complicated program. Unless some miracle happens it will be a couple of weeks."

"Great. Then there's still hope for me!"

Whitney couldn't resist smiling at his unending optimism. "Part of your courting philosophy ought to be learning when to give up."

"Never!"

"Don't blame me, I warned you it's hopeless. But thank you for helping me get a key to the store. I appreciate it."

He stood up and brushed the crumbs off his hands. "Hate to hit the road, but I'm afraid I have to. There's just one thing: take my advice and don't mention this key business to Mr. Prescott or Mr. Stanringham. I don't want any of us to get in trouble. Charlie's too old to be hunting for a new job now."

He turned to go but stopped in the doorway. "Oh, by the way, you'd better call and tell Charlie when you plan to be in the store so he can fix the alarm system. We don't want you busted by the fuzz for breaking and entering, do we?"

"What about the night watchman?"

"No need to have one with our new alarm system. See you tonight. I'll bet those hamburgers of yours will be tastier than a steak broiled over good ol' mesquite wood."

Chapter Seven

By the time Whitney had worked for thirty minutes on the computer her apprehension had almost disappeared. Back in the unthreatening world of numbers and programming symbols she felt safe. An hour later the phone rang. She grabbed the receiver quickly, hoping the call would be from Bradford, but it wasn't.

"Whitney, this is Millicent Hopper. I arrived from Dallas this morning and need to see you right away. I've got such problems you just wouldn't believe! Could you meet me in the fur department?"

Whitney glanced at her watch. "It's almost noon. Are you tied up for lunch?"

"Aren't you?" Millicent demanded.

"Why . . . no, I'm not," Whitney answered, puzzled at her tone. "I thought we could eat and talk at the same time."

"It's a splendid suggestion. Let's do meet for lunch. That plastic food they had the nerve to serve me on the plane this morning would have driven an elephant to diet. I'm starved!"

After a few more rambling comments the fur buyer rang off. Whitney could see how Millicent earned her reputation as a scatterbrain. Yet evidently all that gibberish was an affectation of a very shrewd mind. Lunch should be interesting, Whitney mused, hanging up the phone.

Millicent tried her hardest to find out if Bradford had come back early from Dallas to see Whitney. After fifteen minutes of hedging, Whitney changed her mind. "Interesting" wasn't a strong enough word to describe an encounter with Millicent, she decided, as the torrent of hints, insinuations, and questions continued to pour over her head.

Finally when it became obvious Whitney wasn't going to cooperate, Millicent threw up her hands. "All right, my dear, play those cards close to your chest. I just want to tell you one thing. I liked you the first moment I saw you, and my instincts are usually right on target. So take my advice. You're what Bradford needs. If you haven't already grabbed the dear boy, do it! He's too good a man to lose. If I were a few years younger I'd even give you some competition."

Before Whitney could say anything, Millicent's words tumbled on so rapidly she hardly paused to take a breath. "And another thing. Bradford was so restless while we were in Dallas I thought he was going to wear out his shoes with all the pacing he did. I knew that witch of an ex-wife of his was living there and wondered if she was causing all the to-do, but was I wrong. We ran into her in one of the showrooms, and I thought goody, now the sparks will fly. Sparks? Rubbish! They didn't even set off the briefest flicker. It wasn't a bit fun."

Millicent took a huge gulp of air and rushed on, "When we ran into Frederick Kent, that devilishly handsome buyer from I. Magnin's in San Francisco, Bradford couldn't wait to ask him if he knew you. I knew then that his heart was here. And I'm glad!" Millicent reached out and patted Whitney's hand. "From the look in your eyes you deserve to find happiness as much as he does."

Whitney returned Millicent's warm smile. "Thank you for caring. We'll see."

As she took a spoonful of raspberry mousse, Whitney's hand froze halfway to her mouth. Suddenly one part of Millicent's deluge of words struck her. *Bradford had been asking a buyer in San Francisco about her!* Why? Did he suspect something?

Then her fingers relaxed, and she finished the bite. Bradford cared for her. It was natural he'd ask. Besides, he was probably just making conversation. Yes, that had to be it, she decided, shoving the thought far back in her mind.

"You said you had a problem, Millicent. How can I help?"

Love's Suspect

"It didn't strike me until I was in Dallas what a terrible mess this anniversary sale is going to be. I'm already drowning in paperwork, and the sale hasn't even started yet. And as if that wasn't enough, Raphael Designs is being extremely difficult."

"In what way?"

"My furs are the featured item for week three of the sale. I wanted week two, but Mr. Agajanian snared that with his Oriental rugs. Since my sale merchandise is a consignment order we're working from a dollar amount. I'm not even sure how many coats I'm getting, except I know it will be more than a thousand. I didn't expect to pick specific styles for that many coats, but I did think they'd let me order what kinds of furs I wanted. But in order to get a good selection of fur types, I had to agree to a variable rate of discount. That odious salesman at Raphael Designs knew I had to have coyote fur represented in the consignment. That's why I got saddled with this bookkeeping nightmare! I thought you'd better know all this before you start writing the new program for my department."

Variable discounts—what a programming mess! Whitney tried not to frown. Morgan had warned her that the anniversary sale was the worst possible time to be implementing a new system. This was probably only the first of many complications.

"I'm sure we can work something out," Whitney soothed, sounding happier than she felt. "Why don't we go to your office so I can see the figures?"

In Millicent's office, packing lists and order books battled markdown forms and inventory sheets for a place on the top of her desk. She shoved a pile of catalogues off a chair so Whitney could sit down. "See what I mean?" Millicent gestured to the paper blizzard. "I'm drowning in paper, but that's *my* problem. Here's one for *you.* As I told you Raphael Designs is giving me a different discount for each type of fur. Mink gets cost minus ten percent, Persian lamb six and so on. Confusing, isn't it?"

"Yes, but not impossible. What paperwork comes in with the merchandise? The invoice?"

"No, the invoice is sent later. The only thing that comes with the goods is the packing list." Millicent dug around in the debris on her desk, found a piece of paper, then handed it to Whitney. "Here, look at this. It's the Raphael Designs packing list which came with their last shipment."

The Xeroxed sheet, headed by the Raphael Designs logo, listed style number, quantity per size, and cost. "There aren't any marks. How do you know you received all of these styles? I don't know much about retailing, but shouldn't every item be checked in to make sure there is no shortage?"

"I suppose so," Millicent shrugged, unconcerned. "The first five years I was a buyer I did that religiously. In all that time I found only one mistake, and it was in our favor. I had to send the most fabulous leopard coat back, and that hurt. Now I don't bother unless I have extra time. Of course, what buyer ever has extra time?"

"May I take this packing list so I can get familiar with the way Raphael Designs ships?"

"Certainly. I don't need it. I've been in an absolute dither about this sale, but you've been a big help. I feel worlds better."

"Now maybe you can help me."

"Wonderful!" Millicent's frizzy brown hair bounced about her head as she nodded eagerly. "I'd love to do that. Every spinster adores giving advice on *amour*."

"You are incorrigible." Whitney laughed. "I don't need *that* kind of advice. This is a professional question. Mr. Stanringham wants the new program I'm writing to provide better inventory control. Apparently there have been some serious shrinkage problems."

"There certainly have, and it's been getting a lot worse recently."

"The new program should help. I don't have time to go out to the warehouse and follow the goods from the delivery dock, through all checking in and marking processes. Could you talk me through the procedure? Hopefully I'll be able to spot some ways to control these losses."

Fifteen minutes later Whitney looked down at the notes she'd been taking and shook her head. "It's a wonder the shrinkage isn't worse than it is. Looking at this procedure I can spot ten places either merchandise could be lost or dollars diverted incorrectly in the bookkeeping system."

"I don't want you to get the wrong idea. Our store has tighter security measures than most—Mr. Stanringham insists on that—but it's impossible to control everything." The older woman frowned. "A department store is a thief's paradise. It's bad enough during the regular season, but I shudder when I think what could happen during the chaos of this anniversary sale."

As quickly as Millicent's frown formed it lifted. "Come out on the floor with me. The most incredible coat arrived this morning. I want you to see it."

Casually thrown over the shoulders of a mannekin dressed in a silver lamé ball gown was a full-length lynx coat. "Furs need to be experienced to be appreciated. Here, try it on," Millicent urged, lifting it off the model.

As Whitney slipped into the coat, Millicent added, "I know you liked the fox coat, but I think lynx is even better."

"Oooh, you're right," Whitney agreed, running her fingers through the thick fur. "It feels as soft as a Persian kitten's fur. I may change my mind and wish for one of these instead of the red fox." She lifted her shoulder, drawing the fur up to caress the edge of her chin. "This fur is so luxurious I feel deliciously sinful just touching it."

"I agree. Lynx is a fabulous fur, one of our customers' favorites. I didn't need more, since I had ten already on order coming in at full price, but those scoundrels at Raphael Designs didn't give me any choice. You know, that silvery color is stunning with your dark hair. Go look in the mirror."

Whitney walked to the elegant brass-mounted cheval glass standing near the front of the department. Her smile froze. The mirror caught the glory of the fur; it also caught Morgan Stanringham's scowl. His gaze fell on her like an icy blanket; cold, disapproving—it seemed to be silently saying, "You were hired to sit in front of a computer, not prance around trying on coats you can't possibly afford!"

Quickly she handed the coat back to Millicent. "I have a lot of work to do. I'll see you later."

Whitney didn't need to glance back to know Morgan was watching. His voice caught her one step short of the escalator.

"Miss Wakefield, we have something to discuss. I checked in your office, but obviously you were *out*."

She didn't like his inflection on the word. He might as

well have said "out cavorting," but she refused to apologize for trying on that lynx coat. Making her voice as icily efficient as his, she said, "I'm sorry I missed you. Millicent and I had lunch together to discuss the bookkeeping procedure for her fur consignment. Is there something I can help you with?"

"I want that computer code you and Bradford have decided to use to secure the new program. He forgot to give it to me before he left for Dallas."

"There's no reason to make it complicated, so we decided to use—"

"Not here, for God's sake! Anyone could hear you. Write it down and put it in a sealed envelope. I want it on my desk before you leave." Without waiting for her assent he turned and left.

Whitney couldn't get away from him fast enough as she stepped on the escalator. Her heart was still hammering when she slammed the door to the computer room. Before she'd even had time to take a deep breath the phone shrilled. Earlier she'd reached for it eagerly, expecting to hear Bradford's voice on the line; now her hand hesitated. Would it be another blast from Morgan?

Whitney sighed shakily when she heard Mr. Agajanian's heavy accented request. "Miss Wakefield, might I borrow a piece of your time?"

She forced her fingers to relax their stranglehold on the receiver. "Of course. How can I help you?"

"This weekend, a thought came to me. My rug tickets need one more thing. Is it too late to ask you for a change?"

"No, I haven't started the subroutine for your department yet."

"Ah, that is good for my ears to hear. My rugs come from many areas of the world. If it is not too much trouble to you, might I have the country of origin listed?"

His old-world courtesy soothed Whitney's ragged nerves. By the time she hung up the phone her mood had brightened. The rest of the afternoon sped by as other buyers, also with a weekend of reflection behind them, called with changes they wanted included in the new program for their departments. Between phone calls Whitney wondered idly why Morgan was so insistent on having the code when he claimed he knew nothing about computers, but before she could think about it further Mr. Snyder, the appliance buyer, phoned.

It was close to five o'clock when Whitney pushed her chair back from her desk. After taking a well-earned stretch, she spread the flow chart, showing the plan for the new computer program, out on a table. She was leaning over, making a change in the looping pattern, when she felt hands slide around her waist. Before she could straighten up, Bradford's body molded suggestively to hers, trapping her against the table. A moment later his lips began a nuzzling expedition across the back of her neck.

"This job is just one distraction after another," she murmured, tilting her head so Bradford's kiss could find her ear. "Luncheon dates with nosy buyers, phone calls wanting changes, and now this. How am I ever going to get any work done?"

Bradford sighed, his lips deserting their delightful explorations. When she pivoted in his arms she saw his frown. "What's wrong? You know I was only kidding. I love interruptions from you, especially when they're accompanied by a kiss."

His hands encircled her waist. "I was just thinking what hell the rest of the week is going to be. I'll be lucky to see you at coffee break." He kissed her forehead. "And believe me, after last night, sharing a cup of coffee is definitely not all I had in mind."

"Well, I may have good news. Every time I pick up the phone it's another buyer requesting a change or addition to the program. At this rate I may be here for months."

"Good. It may take me that long to untangle this anniversary sale mess."

"I assume Charlie's news about the truck strike wasn't just a rumor?"

"No, damn it, it wasn't. I've been on the phone all day rerouting the sale merchandise so it can be shipped by rail. The goods start arriving tomorrow, and on top of everything else I have to do, Morgan has put me in charge of the delivery schedule. I'll probably be tied up every night this week. What luck! The truckers go on strike back East, and it means a lot of overtime and headaches for everyone here. It almost seems like this seventy-fifth anniversary sale is jinxed. I wonder what else can happen?"

"Raphael Designs could forget to ship the coyote coats. Then you'd have the truckers plus Millicent on your back," she teased.

He shuddered. "I'm not sure which would be worse! Anyway, it looks as if we're covered for the first week of the sale. Every department has featured items, but the highlight will be a fabulous sale on televisions and video recorders. International Electric has assured me Amos Snyder's merchandise will arrive next week. He drove one helluva hard deal to make this purchase. The discounted price should really pull in the customers. It will be an excellent kickoff for the whole sale."

"From the enthusiasm I hear in your voice, I think you care almost as much about Stanringham's as Morgan."

One arm tightened around her as his other hand moved over her back. "Morgan is obsessed with Stanringham's; little else matters to him. I, on the other hand, have several interests."

She writhed against him, reacting to the wondrously disturbing sensations his hand created as it slipped lower, finally finding the curve of her buttocks and lifting her more intimately against him. "Think of me tonight while you're watching some vintage movie on the late show. While John Wayne is single-handedly saving a whole squadron in the waters of the North Atlantic I'll be scheduling freight shipments."

"Oh, my late show days are over," she answered tartly, stepping aside. "I've invited someone over to dinner."

"Who?"

The harsh rasp to his voice hinted at jealousy, and Whitney couldn't resist playing out the scene a bit longer. Casually studying her nails, she answered, "Eddie."

Bradford was incredulous. "You invited Eddie over to your apartment for dinner?"

"Why not? He likes me, he's young, he's attractive, he's—" When she saw anger turn Bradford's eyes a hard green, she stopped teasing. "He also promised to fix something in the apartment. In return, I said I'd throw some hamburgers on the grill, that's all."

"You'd be a lot safer with a bowl of popcorn and a good B

movie than cooking dinner for Eddie. If I weren't so completely tied up I'd come and chaperone. You may need it!"

"Eddie's just an overgrown kid. He reminds me of an eager puppy that's not quite housebroken yet. Besides, I've been handling his type for years. For me, it's blond-haired men with green eyes that are dangerous."

His smile faded as he drew her into his arms. "This week is going to be hell without you. I'll be trapped here every night while you're at home alone—or worse, while you're there cooking dinner for that overgrown puppy. I'm not so sure Eddie is as harmless as you think. Puppies can turn into wolves! I don't like it." He paused, then nodded. "I have it. Starting tomorrow I'll schedule Eddie for the late driving shift. Then I won't have to worry where he is. Delegating is one of the joys of being an executive!"

"Poor Eddie, you'll ruin all his amorous plans."

"Poor Eddie! What about poor lonely me?"

Whitney wound her arms around his neck, then drew his head down toward hers. "I'd better give you something to sustain you through all that work. I'd hate for you to get so busy you forget about moonlight and gold carpeting, not to mention your Rhett Butler act."

It was a long delightful five minutes before he left. The instant the door closed, oppressive loneliness settled over Whitney. She returned to her desk chair and sank down onto it, but she didn't turn back to the computer. Instead she ran a fingertip over her sweetly bruised lips. Bradford was gone, yet the taste of his kiss lingered on her mouth. Even thinking about the caress of his lips, remembering the arousing rasp of his tongue, sent a ripple of warmth to her very center. Once there the heat concentrated like a slowly building fire, shocking her with the urgent need it stirred. He wasn't even in the room . . . yet she wanted him! The hungry sensations tormented her with their throbbing warmth until she squirmed on the chair seat, trying to find some relief from the tingling demands pulsing through her.

She jumped out of the chair. How had Bradford done this to her in so short a time? No man had ever possessed such a power to move her. As she paced, the memory of their walk by the river replayed in her thoughts. Was this magic between them just the reaching out of two lonely people?

Was it the stirring of new love? Or, anxiety nagged, was it mere desire? Dear God, she silently prayed, it has to be more than a passion's fling. Please let it be more!

The rest of the week proved to be as hectic as Bradford had promised. Whitney's evenings—including the one with Eddie—were uneventful, but her days were chaotic. The only time they could steal to spend together was at coffee break. Those moments became the focus of Whitney's day. She found herself straining to hear his footsteps nearing when she should be plotting the flow chart, dreaming about their walk by the Mississippi when she should be entering data, remembering their night of passion.

Every day she dressed carefully, doing her best to look both professional and alluring. Every day when Bradford came in and closed the door, the pleasure of being together wove an enchanting spell around them. For those all-too-brief moments the rest of the world disappeared, their growing need for each becoming the only reality. But unfortunately some interruption always shattered the spell. Each parting became harder.

Friday morning Whitney plugged in the coffee pot as usual, then sat down in front of the computer. After fifteen minutes a prickling sensation, feeling like a mouse scampering over her skin, brought goose bumps. She'd heard no one approach, but she sensed a malevolent presence.

She shut her eyes a long moment, gathering her courage, then spun the desk chair around to meet the steely hardness of Morgan's gaze. Twice before that week she'd glanced up to find him at the door, watching her work. Those times he had only given a curt nod before moving on. This time he inquired, "How are you coming along with the program?"

Entwining her fingers tightly together to keep them from trembling she answered, "With luck I will have the system operational before your anniversary sale is over, Mr. Stanringham. Would you care for a cup of coffee while we discuss my progress?"

"No, I think not. Thank you for delivering the code so promptly." He glanced around the room. Before she could answer he continued, "It seems odd to find a stranger controlling our computers. They are the heart of Stanring-

Love's Suspect 85

ham's." Abruptly his glance swung back to her. "Who is your superior at Your Program Place? Bradford didn't mention the name when he convinced me to retain your services."

"I report to Mr. Greenwald."

"How long have you been with that firm?"

Before she could answer his probing questions, Bradford appeared at the door. "Good morning, Morgan. Your secretary is looking for you. I'm afraid there's a problem with clearing some of Mr. Agajanian's rugs through customs in New York. The inspector would like to speak with you."

Morgan looked at Whitney, then glanced at the other man. "Bradford, I'll need to see you privately sometime before the meeting this evening." With those curt words, he turned and walked out of the room.

The ominous cloud remained in the room after he'd left. Even Bradford's cheerful smile didn't completely destroy the eerie feeling shrouding Whitney. Luckily her weekly appointment with Mr. Greenwald gave her an escape from the foreboding atmosphere. The meeting was over at three o'clock, but she couldn't face going back to the store. Instead she parked her car near the Gateway Arch and took a long walk along the river before returning to her apartment.

After a barely edible dinner of leftover meatloaf Whitney settled down to work. By midnight she had worked out the subroutine to give Millicent the additional information she'd requested on her price tickets. After pouring a fresh cup of coffee Whitney pulled out her notes of what Mr. Agajanian wanted. A sharp rap on her door sent her pen skidding across the paper, smearing a column of numbers.

She nervously tightened the belt of her cerise kimono as she walked toward the door. "Who is it?"

"Someone urgently in need of a back rub and a nightcap."

The deep baritone voice brought a soft smile to Whitney's lips as she opened the door.

Bradford's glance raked down over her short silk robe and he smiled. "I just happened to be driving by and saw your light on. Since I'm out of brandy I couldn't resist stopping by to see if I could borrow a cup from you."

"A cup of brandy? That's some line you've got!" She glanced at her watch. "Do you know it's after midnight? My reputation will be in shreds. You'd better get in here before you wake up any of my neighbors."

He reached for her the moment the door was closed. "It's been a long day and I'm tired. Want to kiss me awake?"

Her hands came up against his chest to hold off his advance. "If you're that exhausted maybe you should go home and go to bed."

"Sounds boring. You'd hardly expect me to think that was an appealing idea when Miss Scarlett, Mata Hari, and Salome are all here."

"What a fickle man! You're not content with one woman, you want three."

"Only if those three women are you, Whitney. You give me all the variety I can handle."

Bradford's hand tangled in her long hair, gently capturing her head so she couldn't escape.

Long moments later he broke away from the enchantment. His eyes were smoky from the passion they'd shared. "Just as I expected; kissing you is marvelous therapy. I'm wide awake again. How about that brandy you offered?"

"The brandy *I* offered? I thought it went along with the back rub you mentioned."

Bradford rubbed his hands up and down her back; first kneading the tight muscles of her shoulders, then moving down to run strong fingertips across the tingling flesh of her lower back. He smiled when he heard her sharp intake of breath as the caress wandered upward again, brushing her side so that his touch just grazed the sensitive edges of her breasts.

"That's just a sample. The rest of the back rub comes later."

"I thought you were the one urgently in need of a back rub."

"Actually, what I had in mind was a mutual massage session."

"Talk about planning ahead—you've got every detail of this seduction scene already worked out."

His smile faded. "Not really. In fact, I didn't plan to

come here tonight at all, but after the session this evening I wanted to see you."

"I guessed that when you said you just happened to be driving by. My apartment is miles out of your way."

Whitney took his hand, and together they walked toward the sofa. "You relax. I'll get your nightcap."

It took a while to warm the brandy. When Whitney came back into the living room, Bradford's eyes were closed and his head was nestled comfortably against the cushions. A smile touched his lips. He looked so peaceful, at rest with the cares washed away. She stood for a long time, looking down at him, savoring every line, every rugged angle, every precious detail of his face.

Finally with her free hand she curled her fingers around his shoulders and gave a gentle shake. "Bradford, your nightcap is ready."

His eyelids didn't flicker. When she bent nearer to put the snifters on the coffee table, she heard his deep, even breathing. He hadn't exaggerated; even asleep exhaustion shadowed his face.

A few minutes later she returned from her bedroom with a blanket and an extra pillow. A small grunt followed by a contented sigh was his only response as she eased off his shoes, then settled him down on the sofa. Whitney turned to leave but hesitated. Her reluctance to wake him battled the temptation for one last touch. Leaning nearer she let temptation win. For a tantalizing moment she inhaled the unique scent belonging only to him, then placed a loving kiss on his forehead.

Chapter Eight

EARLY the next morning the shrill cawing of a blue jay sitting in a tree outside her window woke Whitney. Dawn's light was just beginning to paint rosy tints across the room as she sat up in bed and stretched. Memories of the night before brought a smile to her lips as she slipped into the cerise kimono and tiptoed into the living room.

Sprawled on the sofa with one arm flung over his eyes, his blond hair ruffled into a dozen cowlicks by sleep, Bradford looked so adorable it took considerable effort not to slide under the blanket beside him. Only remembering how exhausted he'd seemed the night before kept her from waking him. Silently she returned to her bedroom.

Whitney stepped into the shower and turned the hot water on full force, enjoying how good it felt beating down against her bare back. Eyes closed, head tilted back, she let the water stream over her long hair, then stretched out her hand for the shampoo and—

Suddenly two arms wrapped around her naked waist as another body joined her under the spray. Bradford muffled her startled shriek with his mouth. Against her parted lips he murmured, "We wouldn't want the neighbors calling the police, would we?"

The possession deepened as they stood entwined, united by the water pounding down on them. Finally he drew away. "Why didn't you call me, my enticing mermaid? I'm always ready for some good clean fun."

Whitney shook a wet fist at him. "You almost gave me a heart attack, climbing into the shower like that. Didn't you ever see *Psycho*?"

He wiped the water out of her eyes so she could see better. "Don't worry. Look for yourself," he suggested, stepping back as far as the small stall would allow. "You're safe. I'm not carrying a knife."

Her gaze obeyed his suggestion, traveling down over his body in a leisurely inspection. Water glistened like diamonds in the hair curling across his chest, ran down in rivulets over the muscular planes of his stomach, curled around the seductive hardness that made him a man. As her glance swept upward again to meet his, Whitney felt the stirring, ignited by his kiss, explode into desperate desire, creating heat within her hotter even than the steamy water enclosing them in their own misty world.

Her eyes never left him as she reached for the soap, then started rubbing it between her hands until she'd produced a rich creamy lather. "Some hostess I turned out to be. You came for a back rub and never got one. Turn around."

The muscles of his back rippled under her fingertips as she started the massage. Up, down, her hands worked, kneading his shoulder muscles, rubbing the stiffness out of his lower back, sliding around to the front to soap his chest, then moving lower to stroke, tease, entice, until his hand grabbed hers to still the motion.

Bradford turned around to look at her. With the water still streaming over them, he pressed her back against the wall of the shower stall. His hands stroked over her wet body. "Now it's your turn."

She smiled as she held out her hand. "Here's the soap."

"Oh, no. I have a better way." Before she could comment he took the soap, then turned off the water.

Once out of the shower, Whitney reached for a fluffy bath towel, but Bradford's hand stopped her. "You're reaching for the wrong thing. This is all we need," he assured her, lifting a bottle from the dressing table.

Her face flamed when she saw what he was holding. "Baby oil? I use that to take off my mascara."

"Trust me, it has other uses!" A rakish grin spread across his face. "You asked me to turn around; now it's your turn."

The first drops of baby oil felt cool as they dribbled down her back; then his hands, made silky by the oil, began rubbing, and the sensation of coolness turned to heat. The heat spread like a raging wildfire as his hands roamed over her back, her sides, the curve of her waist, then slid around to stroke over and over the taut peaks of her breasts. As each pleasure triggered another, Whitney couldn't keep a moan from escaping.

He leaned over to place a kiss in the hollow between her shoulder blades, then raised his mouth to blow a message of wanting against her flesh. "You give me so much, Whitney. And the more you give the greedier I get."

His hands felt wondrously strong as they grasped her shoulders and turned her to face him. She saw the passion in his eyes, knowing he burned as hotly as she, but it seemed so right, so inevitable, she didn't look away from the consuming, demanding desire she saw there.

"If it's right, passion only grows sweeter."

He trailed a lingering kiss down the warm valley between her breasts, then breathed deeply as if to store the memory of her essence. "I think you may possess enough sweetness to last me a long, long, time."

As she watched he reached for the bottle and poured a few more drops of the oil into the palm of his hand. Her knees quivered with need as his massage spread the warm oil over her stomach, then moved lower, anointing, touching, stroking at her feminine core until with a gasp, Whitney couldn't stand the gentle torment any longer.

She captured his hand, then tugged gently as she turned toward the bedroom. "Bradford, come with me. Let me prove how sweet that pleasure can be."

Bright sunlight was flooding the room when Whitney finally stirred in his embrace. Turning her head on the pillow she saw the tiny smile playing around the corners of his mouth. "You look like the tomcat who's just found the cream pitcher."

"Do you blame me? I've waited a long time to feel this perfectly satisfied." He propped himself up on one elbow. A lazy finger traced the curve of her breast. "Few women love as you do, Whitney—giving totally, responding with no coy inhibitions."

"You sound like an expert. I'm not sure I like that," she fussed with a pretended pout.

"Sorry. My divorce papers didn't include a vow of chastity."

A deep rumbling from Bradford's stomach drowned out her retort

"All right, I can take a hint, breakfast it is." She ruffled her fingers through the thick mat of hair covering his chest. "After all, since I enjoy all the delightful things you think of doing when you do have energy, I have a vested interest in keeping you well fed."

While Whitney concentrated on turning the ham and cheese omelette a perfect shade of brown, Bradford told her about the latest list of presale emergencies that had landed on his desk.

When he stopped speaking she glanced over her shoulder at him. "No wonder you were so exhausted. When you arrived last night you looked as if you'd been through hell."

"This sale is turning the whole store into an asylum; everybody's going a little crazy. But Morgan is the worst of all. Even if it did bring you into my life, I think I was wrong to push him into changing over the computer system at this time. It's given him one more problem to worry about, and he has enough on his mind already!"

She slid the omelette onto a plate and handed it to him. "What's there to worry about? Everything is going extremely well. In fact, I think I'll be able to boot the new system for a trial run sooner than I expected."

"I'll tell Morgan that, but I don't know if that will help. We're back to the same problem. It's not the system he's worried about, it's you."

"Me?" Whitney's hand clenched around the handle of the spatula as the frighteningly familiar chill skidded down her spine again. "Why can't that man leave me alone to do my work!"

"Be reasonable. Your work is critically important to the store. He's concerned, and that also makes him suspicious. He asked me some very pointed questions about your background. There was nothing I could tell him, except that you were sent from Your Program Place. I don't even know where you lived before you came to St. Louis."

He paused, obviously waiting for her to offer more information about her past. The silence, quivering like an overtaut rubber band, stretched between them. Whitney searched the green depths of his eyes, willing the words that explained about the terrors of her past to come, but they wouldn't.

How could she tell him Morgan's instincts and suspicions were correct? The truth about her past meant danger. If Morgan discovered her involvement with the bond theft it would be the end, the end of several things. He'd never trust her to touch Stanringham's computers again. Her first independent assignment and maybe her second career would end in disaster.

As she looked across the table at Bradford, it felt as if a knife twisted in her heart. Would it also mean leaving him? Could she stand losing him?

Whitney swallowed nervously, seeing no way out of the dangerous whirlpool her silence created. That silence was a deception—a deception that lay hidden like a land mine. One misstep and it could explode, destroying the relationship they were building. She couldn't risk that! If she had told Bradford the truth that first day, maybe he could have helped. Now it was too late.

"Sorry it's taken me so long to answer, but I've been trying to control my temper," she lied. "I don't want to blow up at you when it's Morgan who deserves my anger. He has no right to ask any questions about my past! Where I lived before I came here is none of his business. It has no bearing on my ability to handle this programming assignment. Tell him that."

She glanced at the clock. "It's almost eight-thirty. Finish your omelette while I go get dressed." As she walked out of the room she heard his exasperated sigh.

The conversation remained stiffly polite as they drove to Stanringham's. The moment they stepped off the escalator on the third floor, Amos Snyder, the appliance buyer, rushed over and grabbed Bradford's arm. "Thank God, you're here, Mr. Prescott. Only twenty minutes before the store opens, and I got a disaster on my hands! I tell you I ordered a hundred, and there are only ninety in the storeroom! I've been a buyer for forty years, and nothing like this has ever happened to me before. What am I going to do?"

Bradford disengaged his arm from the older man's clawing grasp. "Amos, you can start by calming down and explaining exactly what's wrong. You're not making much sense."

"Calm down!" he shouted, running pudgy fingers over his balding head. "How can I calm down when my department is facing ruin? We'll be hauled up on charges before the Better Business Bureau, I just know it. We may even be sued for false advertising!"

"What's going on here?" Morgan demanded. "I could hear Amos shouting from my office. Why didn't you call me, Bradford? If Stanringham's is going to be sued don't you think I should know about it?"

"Settle down, Morgan. Leave the conclusion jumping to Amos. We don't even know what the problem is."

"The problem is ten missing televisions. I ordered a hundred, I advertised a hundred, but I only have ninety! With the sale starting Monday, I'd call that a disaster, wouldn't you?" Amos fumed. "Today's Saturday and International Electric is closed. I can't even call and get any more delivered before the sale starts. And I haven't checked the number of video recorders yet. They could be short, too."

"Are you sure you counted correctly? That's a lot of cartons. You could have made a mistake."

"You know how particular I am, Mr. Prescott," Amos insisted. "I counted twice, but if you don't believe me, ask Charlie. He carried them up here from the dock and put them in the storeroom." He squared his shoulders manfully. "I shall take the blame for this. I should have counted the stock when it came in Tuesday, but I didn't. You can tell the Better Business Bureau that."

"I really don't think the Better Business Bureau is going to come down on our necks because you're ten televisions short."

"But we advertised a hundred at that special price, and those ads have already appeared in the newspapers," Amos repeated.

"Then mark down some from your regular stock," Morgan ordered. "Stanringham's stands behind its ads." He turned his attention to the other man. "Bradford, I want you to check into this. Probably we were merely shortshipped by the company. God knows it happens enough, but I want to be sure. I don't like the thought that ten televisions might have disappeared out of the warehouse—or for that matter, out of our storeroom here. The last thing we need is a thief suddenly turning up in the middle of our anniversary sale! Check the packing slip, count those video recorders, and get Charlie up here. Since he unloaded them you should talk with him."

"He's at the warehouse today."

"I don't care where he is. Get him!"

Whitney had been standing silently, watching the confrontation. When Morgan stopped the stream of instructions, she suggested, "I can doublecheck the count on the computer. One of the first things I did was link the inventory figures, feeding in from the warehouse, into the master printout. It's still under the old system of accounting, since that part of the new program isn't functional yet, but it will give you the quantity per style number that the warehouse received."

For the first time a grudging glimmer of respect flickered in Morgan's eyes. "That is an excellent idea. It never hurts to have a second check on the inventory figures. Maybe that will help cut down on our shrinkage problems. Bradford, go with her. Run those figures, then bring them to my office when you've got this mess straightened out."

Like a deer sensing danger nearby, her mind flashed an alert as they walked to the computer room. Theft—the thought terrified. A nervous tremor shook Whitney's hands as she booted the warehouse inventory program and punched in the code to pull up the figures they needed. Her glance caught Bradford's smile. He seemed so unconcerned, but she wasn't. She couldn't be!

Once the program started running she turned to him. "You're so calm about this. Aren't you worried that the televisions might have been stolen?"

His fingertip traced the line of her jaw. "I love it when your chin gets this determined tilt! Spirited women have always intrigued me."

Irritated, she pulled away from his touch. "I don't think it's particularly spirited to want to know what's going on. You don't seem very anxious to find out if there's been a theft or not."

"You've been watching too many late night Charlie Chan movies. They've given you the urge to play detective."

"Well, maybe someone needs to. So back to my question. Could the televisions have been stolen?"

"Sure, that's always possible. We've had problems before. The season Miguel Portormo was the hot designer we lost a whole shipment of his collection. There are a dozen places where merchandise can disappear en route to a department store. Take your choice. Maybe they never left the docks in New York. Maybe the trucker needed a new rig and decided to use our televisions for the down payment."

"Have you ever had any employees involved in theft?"

"Hell, yes! Employee theft goes on all the time, but it's usually just small stuff. Although," he grinned, "one time we did have an employee try to smuggle out an antique cuckoo clock under her raincoat."

"Don't tell me. It didn't . . ."

"You guessed it," he laughed, obviously reading her mind. "It cuckooed six o'clock right in front of a security guard."

"Bradford, be serious!"

"I am. Ever vigilant—that's my motto. Haven't you noticed how I'm always watching you? But never fear, between those lecherous glances I've also got my eyes on everyone else. Remember, I've seen those Charlie Chan movies, too. So you want to play detective? Ah so, my pearl of the East, let's imagine how he would handle this."

"With a better accent than yours, that's how," Whitney teased.

"Shhh, don't interrupt a great detective. After all, you're the one who wants to do this. First we must assemble our cast of nefarious suspects—if, indeed, we even have suspects. Let's see. Amos is going to retire next year. Maybe he planned the heist to finance his doublewide trailer in Sun City. Our maintenance manager, Charlie, likes to play the ponies. Maybe his horses have been running last lately and he's in hock to his bookie. Then there's always Eddie. What if he's got his eyes on a new Trans Am? And we mustn't forget Millicent."

"Millicent!"

"Quiet! Maybe she's decided to cut out the middleman and wants the money to start her own chinchilla ranch. Wait," he held up his hand, "best of all, what if Morgan decided to rip off the store? There's a real inside man for you—the president of the company." He bowed, Oriental style. "Well, how did I do?"

She laughed. "No one steals from his own store."

"As Confucius say, a fool jumping to conclusions before learning all the facts can break a leg."

"I don't care what Confucius says. I say there's no percentage in stealing from yourself."

"That would be true *if* Morgan owned Stanringham's."

"But I thought . . . I assumed Stanringham's belonged to him."

Bradford grew sober. "Stanringham's was a family-owned business until five years ago when Morgan's father sold out to the Hudson Company. Since Morgan's father held the stock in his name, all the money went to him. From the stories filtering back from Monte Carlo there may not be much left when the roulette wheel stops spinning. Anyway, after he retired, Morgan became president. I was joking about Morgan stealing from the store, but I can see where it might be a temptation. His job's none too secure."

"Why? I heard he's one of the most innovative merchants in St. Louis."

"He is, but that doesn't always keep the cash registers humming. The problem started two years ago when the recession hit. It's no secret Hudson has been unhappy with our profit statements lately. Just between you and me, this anniversary sale may be Morgan's last chance to hang onto his job. That's why he's so anxious that nothing goes wrong—and that brings us right back to those missing televisions."

The clatter of the printer, typing out the information she'd requested, interrupted them. Whitney ripped off the sheet, glanced at it, then handed it to him. "Looks like Charlie Chan can mark this one case closed. Stanringham's was short-shipped. The warehouse received only ninety of each item. We'd better go tell Amos."

Bradford held open the door for her. "I'm sure you're right, but I still want Charlie to confirm the count."

The instant they entered the appliance storeroom, Amos cried, "I knew it! We're short ten video recorders too."

Bradford gave the old man's shoulders a reassuring pat.

"Mr. Prescott, what's the trouble?" Charlie asked as he entered the storeroom. "They told me to hightail it over here."

"It's just something we need to check on, Charlie. You picked up Amos's sale merchandise. Do you remember how many televisions and video recorders you loaded?"

"There were ninety of each," Charlie answered without hesitation.

"Are you sure? That was several days ago."

"Look, Mr. Prescott, when someone pays me to do a job I do it right. The packing slip said there were ninety televisions. I loaded ninety, and I put ninety into this storeroom. I counted every blasted one of them."

"All right, Charlie, keep that famous red-haired temper of yours under control. I know you do an excellent job. Where did you put the packing list?"

"There was a whole bunch of stuff on top of Mr. Snyder's desk. I just tossed it on the pile."

Amos looked through the papers on his desk, then shook his head. "It's not here. I asked my assistant to straighten up the office yesterday. He probably threw it out."

"I guess we don't need it. The computer and Charlie agree. International Electric simply short-shipped us. Morgan will be glad to hear there's no thief operating in the store. Amos, you'd better also mark down ten video recorders from stock."

After reporting to Morgan, Whitney and Bradford walked to the computer room. He kicked the door closed and drew her into his arms. "I'm afraid that massage this morning is going to have to last us for a while. I'll be lucky to get down here even for a coffee break next week."

"You don't have to work tomorrow, do you? How about taking a picnic lunch out by the river?"

"The only way we can share a picnic lunch tomorrow is if you bring it to the store."

"But tomorrow's Sunday," she protested.

"I know, but it's not going to be a day of rest for me. There's too much to do. And I don't even want to think what next week is going to be like. At least I won't have to worry about Eddie showing up on your doorstep for hamburgers. He and Charlie are working overtime too."

Bradford pulled away so he could look at her. "You

know, I could quit Stanringham's. I've always had an urge to try my hand at acting."

"You wouldn't do that. I've watched the way your eyes light up when you're talking about the store. You'd miss the excitement of retailing."

"Excitement? Is that what you call it? It's been more like insanity lately."

"Yes, and you love it."

"Maybe, but then there are days I'd quit in a minute if I could afford to. Know where I can lay my hands on some quick bucks?"

"No, but if you find a place let me know. Millicent showed me a lynx coat I'd give anything to have! The fur felt like—"

A sharp knock on the door interrupted her. Whitney raised her voice. "Yes, what is it?"

"Is Mr. Prescott in there with you?" Martha inquired. Whitney opened the door.

"Mr. Prescott, Mr. Stanringham has been calling for you. The first shipment of Mr. Agajanian's rugs has arrived at the warehouse. After the shortage that showed up this morning he wants you there when they're unloaded."

"The next thing I know, he'll be asking me to ride shotgun on the delivery trucks! Whitney, I'm sorry, I've got to go." He leaned nearer and lowered his voice so only she could hear. "My shower is going to be damned lonely tomorrow morning."

Whitney spent Sunday morning cooking. Potato salad, fried chicken, baked beans, strawberry shortcake; as she finished each item she packed it into a picnic hamper. A few minutes before noon she took the bottle of white wine out of the refrigerator, nestled it next to the salad, and closed the lid. When she rang the bell at the employees' entrance, Eddie unlocked the door.

A huge grin spread across his face when he saw her. "Hey, what a great idea. You brought me lunch! Couldn't resist spending some time with me, could you? I knew you'd finally come around."

"Sorry, my friend, but I believe the lady is here to see me," Bradford commented dryly, walking out of a nearby office.

"It figures," Eddie sighed dramatically. "The top brass always walks off with the dames. It was the same in the navy. The officers always got the best girls. Where do you want those round racks moved, Mr. Prescott?"

"To the designer sportswear department."

"Whatever you say. At time and a half I'll move them anywhere you want." With a cheerful wave he sauntered off.

Bradford took her arm. "Will my office be all right, or would you rather eat somewhere else?"

Whitney refused to let anything spoil the day. Shoving the memories connected with that rosewood kidney-shaped desk far back in her mind, she answered gaily, "Since I can't have the Mississippi River for a scenic backdrop it doesn't matter where we eat."

As Bradford watched her spread out a blanket on the carpet of his office and then begin emptying the hamper, he commented, "I don't believe it. You thought of everything—even a corkscrew for the wine. Of course, it isn't the Greek dinner you promised, but it will do."

After munching his way through the last chicken leg, he leaned over and kissed her on the nose. "I wish this picnic could last all afternoon, but—"

"But you have to get back to work. I don't necessarily like it, but I do understand. Oh, well, I might as well work tonight, too. Why don't you carry the picnic hamper down to the employees' entrance for me while I stop in the computer room and pick up some papers I need."

The thick carpet of the furniture department muffled her footsteps as she started back toward the employees' entrance from the computer room. As she approached she heard Morgan's strident words echo through the deserted store. "I don't like it, Bradford! What is she doing here?"

Whitney's stomach lurched when she realized they were talking about her. Instinctively she dodged behind the brocade hangings of a canopy bed so they wouldn't see her.

"Calm down, Morgan. She might hear you."

Morgan's voice lowered to an angry hiss. "You didn't answer my question. Why is she here?"

"Whitney brought me lunch. I know the sale's starting tomorrow, but I still have to eat."

Love's Suspect 101

"Look, Bradford, she already knows too much. I don't want to find her prowling around here after-hours again."

"Don't worry, everything is under control. Nothing is going to go wrong."

"It had better not." After firing those curt words at Bradford, Morgan turned and marched off.

The menace of Morgan's words blanketed Whitney like an icy shroud. She clutched the bed hangings, waiting for her heart to stop pounding, but before she had time to gather her wits Bradford poked his head around the carved bedpost.

"How much of the boss's tirade did you hear?"

Whitney kept her hands hidden behind the heavy brocade fabric so he couldn't see their trembling. "I didn't hear very much," she lied. "Morgan sounded so furious! He acts like he's ready to fire me, and I don't understand why. I'm doing my job, and I'm doing it very well. Why can't he leave me alone?"

Bradford's fingers worked in soothing strokes through her dark hair as he reassured her. "Forget what you heard. Morgan is uptight about the sale, that's all. It was a gamble to stage this huge a sale, especially with the local economy in the doldrums. Remember, millions of dollars in profits are at stake here, plus his reputation is on the line. It's no wonder he's worrying about every detail."

Driving home, Bradford's reassurances replayed in Whitney's thoughts. What he'd said made sense. She was simply overreacting because the job meant so much to her future.

Whitney's chin lifted. Besides, why was she worried? Morgan's feelings, even his suspicions, couldn't affect the success or failure of her project. Her ability controlled that . . . nothing else!

Chapter Nine

A QUIVERING expectancy hung in the air the next morning as Whitney hurried into the store. Like the eerie calm before a thunderstorm, everything seemed suspended, waiting for the opening chimes to ring, kicking off the biggest sale in Stanringham's seventy-five-year history. Whitney had worked late the night before and had unfortunately overslept. When those opening chimes rang, instead of being safe in her office drinking coffee she got caught in the middle of the first floor.

Whitney's eyes widened as she watched the stampede of shoppers charging straight at her. Before she could dodge behind a counter the maelstrom of bargain hunters swept her into the fray as they grabbed for cashmere sweaters, fought over eelskin purses, pawed through the racks of silk dresses. Finally, after being crushed against the sharp edge of the jewelry counter by an aggressive shopper reaching for some specially imported cultured pearls, Whitney managed to escape.

Battered, bruised, with stockings torn, she limped into the computer room. "What happened to you?" Bradford demanded as he handed her a cup of coffee. "You look like you lost an argument with a bus."

"Your customers are what happened to me! People see the word *sale* or *marked down* and go absolutely insane!"

"We love that insanity. It means big dollars for Stanringham's."

Whitney patted the top of the computer screen. "I used to think it would be exciting to be in retailing, but I'll take this quiet computer anytime. It doesn't kick, shove, or trample. If you want to find me this week, just look here. I'm not venturing out into that madness again if I can help it."

"Not even for lunch? We may not be able to share an intimate picnic in the beautifully scenic environs of my office, but at least we'd be together."

"May I have an armed escort through those hordes of bargain-snatching marauders?" she teased. "If I get any more bruises, I'll start looking like a zebra." Her brown eyes suddenly glinted with excitement. "But I'd be a successful zebra!"

He blinked. "Excuse me?"

"Last night was incredible! I was working on the subroutine that controls the open-to-buy report, and suddenly it all clicked."

"What clicked?"

"A way to save Stanringham's several hundred thousand dollars a year."

"Several hundred thousand dollars!" he whistled. "If you pulled that off we should forget the coffee and break out the champagne."

"Not during business hours, please. Champagne makes my head fuzzy." She laughed, springing to her feet. The excitement of what she'd accomplished made sitting still impossible. Her step held an enthusiastic bounce as she paced around the small room. "I thought when I first printed out the open-to-buy report that it took too long to run. Last night when I started checking those subroutines I discovered the original programmer had made it needlessly complicated. So," she brushed off her hands, "I worked out a method which significantly reduces the number of steps. You know how expensive computer time is. Since this particular program runs weekly, making it run a whole lot faster should save Stanringham's a bundle over the year!"

Bradford raised his coffee mug to her in salute. "I become more impressed each moment I spend with you. I know enough about programming to realize what a coup you just scripted. You deserve a bonus!"

"My bonus is solving the problem. No amount of money can ever equal that thrill. It's the ultimate high."

"What a slam to my ego!" he complained, pretending to sulk. "And I thought it was my Rhett Butler act that put those smoldering sparks in your brown eyes."

Love's Suspect

"Correction," she quickly interrupted. "Solving a programming problem is only *one* way I experience that ultimate high."

"Thanks, ego mender. I'll tell Morgan what you've done."

She grimaced. "You can tell him, but I doubt it will make any difference. He doesn't like me."

"Well, then he's a fool!" Bradford glanced at his watch. "I'm running behind. Let's plan something special for this weekend. Even Morgan can't expect me to work two Sundays in a row." He paused at the door. "Remember, we're meeting for lunch."

"I'll be right here waiting. I'm not going out into that horde of shopping sharks again if I can help it!"

"That's hardly a nice way to describe Stanringham's valued customers!" he protested with a laugh. "See you at noon."

Two hours later her phone rang. Irritation crackled through Bradford's voice. "I have to cancel our luncheon plans. There's another shipping crisis with Mr. Agajanian's carpets—another problem with customs. I swear the next time we decide to import a collection of antique and one-of-a-kind Oriental carpets I'm asking for a leave of absence. Some other idiot can handle it. I'm sorry, Whitney."

That change of plans was only a prelude to the chaos of the rest of the week. On most days Bradford didn't even have time to drop in for a cup of coffee. Hurried phone calls were an unrewarding substitute for being with each other. For Whitney those days when she didn't see him seemed painted in shades of gray. As she sat hour after hour, undisturbed at the keyboard, she found only one good thing about the situation: she was accomplishing a prodigious amount of work.

She was so excited about the way the programming was progressing that she arrived forty-five minutes early Wednesday morning. When she unlocked the door to the computer room she gasped. A figure was bending over the computer.

"Mr. Stanringham! What are you doing here?"

"It's my store. I have a right to be anywhere I wish and to check on any aspect of the business I wish."

"Certainly, but . . ." Confused, she let the words fade.

As Whitney glanced at the screen full of numbers, the disarranged paperwork on her desk, then back to Morgan, the words he spoke at their first meeting echoed clearly. "The only thing I know about computers is how to read the open-to-buy . . ." If that were true, why was he here running the computer and going through her papers? And if it weren't true, why did he lie?

She swallowed nervously, suddenly glad she'd left the door ajar. Before she could say anything, he commented, "As long as I am here, why don't you give me your midweek progress report. It will save you a trip to my office." His words were coldly clipped. "I want to know what you'll be working on the rest of this week."

Whitney dug around in her briefcase, found the correct folder, and handed it to Morgan. With a curt nod, he left. Yet even as the door closed his presence lingered. She tried to figure out what he'd been doing at the computer, but nothing made sense. She tried shoving the mystery aside by reaching for a chart showing a looping pattern, but she couldn't concentrate. The questions wouldn't be banished. What had Morgan been doing? Why did he always make her feel so uneasy? It was midmorning before she was able to force the uneasy confusion away and return to work.

No one else disturbed her during that day or the next. To her delight, by the time she turned off the computer on Thursday night, she realized the series of subroutines controlling the inventory report would be ready for its first run the next day.

Friday morning she again arrived at Stanringham's early, partly to avoid the shoppers' riot and partly because she was eager to see how her inventory program would run. But when she reached the computer room door her hand hesitated to turn the knob. Would Morgan be inside?

She took a deep breath, then pushed the door open. She was slowly letting it out when something grabbed her attention. The fragrance of fresh-brewed coffee filled the office, telling her Bradford had already arrived, but it was the enormous jar of olives sitting by the computer that caught her eye. She looked around expecting to find a note of explanation from him, but there wasn't one. What a strange thing for him to leave.

An hour later a knock interrupted her final check on the

looping patterns for the subroutines of the program. She glanced up to find Eddie leaning against the doorjamb, holding a paper bag.

"What a nice interruption. I've been feeling neglected. You haven't brought me almond croissants or even a cinnamon roll in over a week."

"Give the blame to Mr. Stanringham, not me. He's kept me so busy I haven't even had time to give my car her weekly wash."

She nodded toward the bag in his hand. "Will you join me for breakfast? There's fresh coffee."

"Nope, I'm changing my strategy again. From now on I'm going to play hard to get, so don't expect any more croissants. I've tried everything else. Maybe being unavailable will make me irresistible to you. Anyway, I'm only the delivery boy. Mr. Prescott asked me to bring this package to you. I don't even know what's in it." He wrinkled up his nose in distaste. "But I'll tell you one thing, whatever it is, it smells funny!" He thrust the bag at her. "Here, you open it while I stand back."

Whitney frowned as she took the bag. Carefully she opened it, looked in, then laughed when she saw the wedge of white odoriferous cheese. "It's just feta cheese, Eddie. It may smell a little funny, but it tastes delicious! The goat's milk they use in Greece gives it quite a unique flavor. You should try some sometime."

He shook his head so vigorously his red hair stood on end. "Goat's milk! Forget it. Not even you are going to get me to try that stuff. I'll stick to good old American cheese. Why is Mr. Prescott sending you a hunk of that weird-smelling cheese anyway?"

She smiled, remembering the Greek dinner she'd promised Bradford. Greek olives, feta cheese . . . now she knew where his hints were leading. "It's just a private joke, Eddie." Changing the subject she asked, "What are your plans for this weekend?"

"That's supposed to be my line. I can't make my plans until I know what you're doing. I'm keeping Saturday night open in case—"

"Eddie," she interrupted, "you must understand. I like you, you know that, but liking doesn't mean I'm planning to accept a date with you."

His burly shoulders raised in a resigned shrug. "Oh, all right, but you can't blame a guy for trying to impress the classiest lady who's walked into Stanringham's in a long spell. And I'm not giving up." With a cheerful smile he turned and left the office.

Whitney glanced at the jar of olives, then reached for the telephone to call Bradford to invite him to the dinner she'd promised to cook.

His secretary answered. "I'm sorry, Mr. Prescott isn't in his office. The shipment of Oriental rugs has arrived from the warehouse. He is with Mr. Agajanian making the final arrangement for their display."

With a sigh she hung up the phone and turned on the computer to make a few final corrections. Another knock interrupted. This time when she turned around she saw Charlie standing at the door.

"Charlie, I'm glad you're here. A dozen times I intended to call you to thank you for getting the key to the store for me, but then I'd get busy and I'd forget." Her smile asked for his understanding.

"Don't worry your pretty head about it. I'm always glad to help. Just remember, don't tell the boss about it, or we'll be meeting at the unemployment office."

Whitney winked at him. "The key will be our secret, I promise."

"Good. Now on to the reason I've come visiting. I've got something for you." He held out a gaily wrapped parcel. "I was toting up some of those rugs to Mr. Agajanian's department, and Mr. Prescott asked me to deliver this package to you. I said, 'with pleasure!' Visiting a beautiful lady is more fun than unloading trucks. But since that's what they pay me for, I guess I'd better get back to work."

As the wrapping paper parted, she laughed out loud. Inside she saw a white bed sheet and a note, scrawled in Bradford's bold handwriting, reading, "Do it yourself toga kit."

She was on her feet, ready to search for him, when he appeared in the doorway.

"Okay, I've had it with subtle hints," he insisted in mock anger. "I thought you were a bright lady, but obviously I need to be more direct if I don't want to starve.

Here, maybe this will jog the memory of a promise you made," he said, tossing a book to her.

"Cooking the Greek Way," Whitney read aloud. "I seem to have some vague recollection about Greece." With eyes widened in innocence, she commented, "Ah, I remember. Didn't you promise to take me to a Greek restaurant for dinner?"

"I warn you, tease a man starving for dolmathes and you may bring the wrath of Zeus down on your head."

She threw up her hands in defeat. "Okay, you win, I'll cook. I certainly don't want trouble with the gods. Actually, I called you this morning to invite you for a Greek feast tomorrow night. Didn't you get my message?"

"No, I've been tied up."

When he picked up the bed sheet a gleam flashed in his green eyes. "I can't wait to see you in your toga."

"Sorry, I can't serve a Greek meal in a toga."

"Why not?" His gaze wandered down over her body as he visualized, "One shoulder bare, the sheet draped so I get glimpses of your bare thigh every time you take a step . . . a toga sounds good to me!"

"If I wore that we'd never make it past the appetizers, and you know it. Besides, that's not my point. I can't serve a Greek dinner in a toga because that's what the Romans wore. Greeks wore himations."

"I knew I shouldn't have tangled with someone as intelligent as you are. You always thwart my lecherous designs."

Whitney took the sheet from his hands, dropped it on the desk, and wound her arms around his neck. "If I'm as intelligent as you say, would I do that? Thwarting your lecherous designs would ruin my fun along with yours. Trust me, I don't think I can come up with a himation, but I will find something scandalously risqué to wear."

"I may forget the dolmathes and take *you* for my appetizer!"

His embrace claimed her, molding her body tightly against him. The warmth of his powerful body began stirring the embers of desire, embers she knew would explode into passionate flames the next evening. His lips, his tongue, stroking, nibbling, tasting of her, entwined with the response she returned willingly, sealing the promise of those pleasures to come.

After they shared a quick lunch together, Whitney went back to the computer room. Two final adjustments finished the inventory part of the program. She stood for a long moment looking at the end product of a lot of her work, then, with fingers crossed, punched the button, starting the printout.

Would it run correctly? Had she forgotten to include some critical subroutine? Would the numbers correlate? Knowing that the possibilities for error were almost endless forced question after question into her mind. As the printer began to type out the rows of numbers she twisted her fingers into a hard knot, waiting.

This is ridiculous, Whitney decided, deliberately relaxing her grip. Watching the printer crank out numbers for an hour wasn't going to make the program run any smoother. After making one more silent wish that everything would work she left the computer room.

The shopping frenzy had quieted to mild pandemonium. She walked by the crowd clustered around a table featuring a collection of specially priced silk scarves and on toward the designer dress department. When Millicent saw Whitney approaching she quickly jammed a mink hat on a head form, then moved to intercept her.

The older woman clapped her hands gleefully as she insisted, "I knew it. I knew you'd be back for that lynx coat! It works every time. Once you've run your fingers through that sinfully lush fur, you're lost."

Whitney laughed at her enthusiasm. "Not me. A lynx coat is definitely not on my shopping list today. I'm looking for a special dress to wear to a dinner party."

"I'll bet it's a dinner party for two!"

"Now, why would you say that, Millicent?"

"There's no fooling these old eyes. I've seen Bradford running around the store these last few days with that silly grin on his face. Once I even heard him whistling to himself as he walked past my department. Only you could have made him look that happy. I'll come with you to look for that dress. I love helping other people spend their money."

As they walked down the marble aisle, Millicent continued, "What kind of dress do you need? Where is the dear boy taking you to dinner?"

"Actually, I've promised to cook him a Greek dinner at my apartment."

"A romantic dinner flavored with the magic of the Greek isles. Say, this is sounding better and better all the time. And I know just the dress you need." Millicent took her arm to urge her forward. "Hurry up, I can't wait to show it to you. Believe me, this gown is a real show stopper: virginal white and sexy as sin. I saw the couture buyer hanging it on the rack last week. For one wild moment I was even tempted to try it on myself, but then sanity returned. It's for beautiful young things, not wizened spinsters like me."

Like a conjurer producing a rabbit, Millicent whipped the gown off the rack and held it up for Whitney's inspection. Whitney gasped in delight. If she'd designed the gown herself it couldn't be any more perfect. It even had the Grecian simplicity of a himation.

"Try it on," Millicent urged.

Whitney reveled in the feel of the silk crepe flowing over her skin as she pulled the gown on over her head. Before she had the last button buttoned, Millicent was knocking on the dressing room door, wanting to see how the dress looked on her.

Whitney pirouetted for her inspection. As the soft pleats floated back in place around her ankles, Millicent raved, "That dress was *made* for this dinner party! It hugs all the right places. Those bugle beads on the shoulder strap make your skin seem translucent. And it even leaves the other shoulder bare in tribute to the ancient Greeks. Buy it!"

"You're right, it is perfect. I think it would be arguing with destiny not to get it." Whitney looked at the price tag and gulped. "Destiny had better appreciate this. Even with my discount, I can just barely afford it."

"Oops, I've got to run. There comes Mrs. Jacobs, one of my best customers. I need to pique her interest in those Raphael Design furs that are on the way. Enjoy that dinner!"

Whitney had changed and was walking toward the waiting saleslady when Eddie arrived. He let out a low whistle when he saw the dress in her hand. "What would it take to convince you to wear something like that for me?"

"I don't think this dress would fit in with the Country and Western crowd," she commented as she handed the gown to the saleslady, then got out her checkbook.

"We wouldn't have to go to the Red Dog Saloon. To get to see you in that dress, I'd spring for a dinner at some fancy restaurant. All you have to do is say the word."

"I'm afraid the word is still no, Eddie."

Even after the rejection he refused to leave her side while she wrote the check, then pulled out her driver's license for identification. Before she could protest he lifted the license out of her hand. "Hey, this is a pretty good picture of you. Do you think I could get a copy for my billfold?"

"Eddie, you're acting like a sixteen-year-old, and I'm getting bored with the act. Will you please give my driver's license to the clerk so she can write the number on the check?"

She expected him to look crushed by her scolding, but his grin seemed even cockier than usual. "Mr. Prescott is one helluva lucky man. Tell him I said so. See you around."

The computer had finished its printout by the time Whitney returned to her office. She looked at the bottom figure then squeezed her eyes tightly shut, trying to control the sudden queasy feeling kicking at her stomach. A one-hundred-and-seventy-five-thousand-dollar differential. How could she be off that far?

Her hands trembled as she laid the inventory report run on the old system next to hers. There was no mistake. Her figures showed Stanringham's had close to two hundred thousand dollars more inventory than shown under the old system. She'd made a colossal error somewhere in the programming. She'd have to retrace every entry to find her mistake.

She was still shaking her head over the mess when Bradford poked his head in the door. When she caught the motion she hastily shoved the two sets of papers into her briefcase before he could see the disaster.

He nodded toward her briefcase. "Ah, I caught you. From the guilt written all over your face I suspect you are

Love's Suspect 113

planning to sneak out of the store before the closing chimes. You must be in a hurry to get home."

"Well, I do have a lot of work to do in the kitchen before tomorrow night, you know. It takes a long time to stuff grape leaves, so I thought I'd leave a few minutes early. You won't tell Morgan, will you?"

Bradford took the briefcase out of her hand and tossed it aside. "I'll keep silent for a kiss."

"Sounds fair," she murmured, walking into his embrace willingly. Neither was breathing evenly when they let the kiss slip away. The green in Bradford's eyes flamed to emerald as he murmured, "You bewitch me, Whitney. I can't even think clearly when I'm with you. Each time I touch you is sweeter than the last and harder to draw away from. Tomorrow night seems like an eternity away."

"There's always tonight," she suggested, tracing the rugged thrust of his cheekbones with her fingertips.

"Tonight, instead of exploring the delights of that gorgeous body of yours, I'll be representing Stanringham's at a convention of kids involved with Junior Achievement. It's a worthy program, but it can hardly compete with you!"

Whitney's thoughts wound about Bradford as she drove home, and unconsciously she started humming a song from *Gypsy.* But how could she drive along humming merrily when the program was in so much trouble her job might even be in jeopardy? With that huge differential staring her in the face she shouldn't feel that everything was coming up roses . . . yet she did. It was totally irrational, but that's what Bradford did for her. He made any thorns feel like roses. Thinking about him possessed the power to fade her troubles until they seemed unimportant. He meant so much to her. When he wasn't there she felt out of kilter. It wasn't just his kisses she missed; she also missed the laughter they shared, talking for hours about everything and nothing, his understanding how she could get so excited over solving a programming problem, the touches given in friendship, not just passion. An endless list.

Suddenly realization struck. The joy when he was with her, the loneliness when he wasn't, the aching need for his touch, everything about the roller coaster ride her emotions were on pointed to one thing. She loved Bradford!

Once acknowledged, Whitney couldn't deny that love. Love had come so softly she hadn't even been aware it was nestling firmly, permanently, into her heart. Now it was too late.

With a choking sob hot tears came. Damn the past! The vice-president of Stanringham's couldn't have a suspected thief for a wife any more than a banker could. Her mind conjured the scene if Bradford ever found out the truth. The look of distrust she'd seen in Douglas's eyes transferred to his, the inevitable words of farewell he'd say, the cold empty future without him. He must never know! Losing Douglas hurt, but she'd survived. With Bradford the feelings plunged so much deeper, touched so many more levels, she didn't know if she could survive the pain of losing him.

Loving him made everything worse. Instead of a shadow, her past loomed like an impenetrable barrier between them. As she turned into the parking lot of her apartment, logic suggested the solution was simple—tell Bradford the truth about her past. The fear of losing him was irrational, she knew that, but realizing that fact had no power to ease the anguish choking her every breath.

The past had long tentacles, tentacles holding her, hurting her. Bradford was ambitious. He wouldn't have risen this high without that drive. Power and success—they were the most seductive of all mistresses. As Whitney walked wearily into her apartment she knew she was powerless to fight them. Douglas had been possessed by that same type of ambition, and she'd lost him. How could it be any different this time?

Silence offered the only hope. Silence! Silence! Silence! The word etched itself into her mind over and over again as she started making out the shopping list for their Greek dinner.

Chapter Ten

THE next morning Whitney's search for some Kefalotyri cheese to use in a stuffed fillo appetizer took her down into one of the eclectic neighborhoods near the Arch. Small shops, fascinatingly diverse, featured everything from handmade Spanish guitars to Indian embroidered silk. As she walked along the sidewalk toward the Greek market, a splash of color caught her eye. When she stopped for a closer look though the window of the shop, called Nostalgia, a mischievous smile touched her lips.

"If Bradford can hint, so can I." She chuckled to herself as she walked through the doorway into the shop and pointed to the wall. "I'll take that poster."

"Ah, another old movie buff." The man smiled fondly at the huge cardboard-backed poster as he lifted it down. "Rhett Butler carrying Scarlett up that sweeping staircase at Tara. Yes, this has to be one of the greatest scenes ever filmed."

Once back in her apartment, Whitney stripped off the brown wrapping paper, then hid the poster in the closet. She wanted to find the perfect moment to spring the surprise on Bradford.

As she started for the kitchen her glance fell on her briefcase, and the smile died. There were so many possibilities for error she hadn't really expected the program to run perfectly the first time, but to have such an enormous discrepancy in the two inventory figures was disastrous! Her first independent assignment, and she'd botched it, botched it badly.

With a determined shake of her head Whitney shoved the briefcase behind the sofa. She was confident she could fix it, but it was going to take time. Monday would be soon enough to start thinking about the problem. She smiled. "Scarlett, you had the right idea! Tomorrow is another day." Tonight meant too much to her. Nothing was going to ruin it, not a hundred-and-seventy-five-thousand-dollar differential or fears that the past might destroy her future!

Hours later Bradford's knock sent her flying eagerly to answer the door. The traces of strain behind his smile of greeting vanished when she stepped fully into view. The sage-green of his eyes fired hotly as his gaze raked over her, taking in every detail of her clinging gown.

"Now I understand why the Greeks attacked Troy. If Helen looked anything like you even I'd go to war to claim such a prize!"

His embrace swept around her, drawing her hard against the muscled length of his body. "I'm glad there's no Hector I have to fight to win you," he whispered against her dark, fragrant hair.

The only sound in her apartment for long moments was the thick plop plop of the soup simmering on the stove. Finally, after the pleasure given and returned by the caress of lips, the moist thrust of tongue meeting tongue, the touch of hands, the savoring of each other's bodies had sated their first explosive passion, Bradford deserted the enticement of her mouth to taste the flesh of her bare shoulder. His teasing bites sent a shudder of aching need through Whitney. Yet when his fingers began undoing the buttons marching down the back of her gown, she pulled away.

"I thought you were only kidding about having me for your appetizer tonight," she protested, bringing her hands up against his chest to hold him off.

"I never kid about the desire you stir in me, Whitney. You're like the finest French cognac, dangerously intoxicating, but so delicious I have no power to resist indulging in the temptation of sampling."

"Couldn't that sampling wait? I spent all day in the kitchen, and I would hate to have all that time wasted. Reheating Greek food is never very successful. Would it stiffen your resistance to me if I offered you some of those dolmathes I promised?"

"It might. I hope what you've planned for dinner is high

in energy value." He winked. "After all, there are many hours to enjoy between now and the dawn. What are we having tonight?"

"Besides the dolmathes we're having tyropitakia, soupa avgolemono, tsouoreki, spanakopita, shrimp Gianni, baklava, and Kokineli."

"On second thought, I think I'll order a pizza!"

"You do, and I'll share that bottle of Kokineli with Eddie."

"Ah well, I guess I'll have to make the sacrifice. Eddie's too young to handle a temptress like you. I just have one question. There isn't octopus hidden somewhere in the jumble of Greek you spouted at me, is there? I'm not into eating tentacles."

"No, you're safe. Come on into the kitchen and see." As Whitney lifted lid after lid she explained, "To translate, we're having stuffed grape leaves, fillo triangles filled with cheese, egg-lemon soup, sesame seed bread, spinach pie, shrimp, a honey and walnut dessert, and a resinous Greek wine."

"Sounds like it might be edible."

"I slave all day preparing a feast worthy of the gods, and you say it *might* be edible! How dare you?" she teased, brandishing a wooden spoon at him.

"I dare because I love to see the way your eyes shoot off those dazzling sparks when you get angry." His hands, moving down her spine in a possessive sweep, didn't stop until they had reached the curve of her fanny. Giving it a playful pat, he ordered, "Just be sure and keep a little of that fire for later this evening."

The candles sputtered low in their sockets when they finally pushed back from the table. Bradford's kiss licked the final traces of the honeyed baklava from her lips. "How about some of that brandy you offered the other night? This time I won't fall asleep, I promise."

Whitney expected to see a relaxed smile on his face once they were settled on the sofa with the brandy snifters, but instead a frown creased his forehead. "All right, what is it?" she demanded. "That meal should have mellowed you, instead I get a frown. There's something wrong. I can see it in your eyes. Did something happen this afternoon during your meeting with Morgan?"

"I wasn't going to bring this up tonight, but maybe I'd better. The problem isn't going to go away, unfortunately. As you guessed, Morgan is on one of his famous terrors. You know he's never been happy about my decision to hire you, but I thought he'd eventually accept it. He hasn't. Ever since last Sunday, when he found you in the store, he's been asking all sorts of questions about your background and your experience. This afternoon he demanded answers."

Whitney raised the snifter to her lips, trying to hide the feeling of panic clutching at her. She swallowed hard, but it didn't help. The tremor in her voice betrayed her as she stammered, "What did you tell him?"

"I told him not to worry, that I only hire the best."

"Thanks for that vote of confidence." She managed a wan smile. "I guess that means everything's all right."

"No, it's not all right! I thought I could put this out of my mind, at least for tonight, but I can't." He sat the snifter down on the coffee table with such force some of the brandy splashed out. "Morgan's questions forced me to face something I've been trying to ignore. Something's going on, and I want to know what it is."

"Nothing is going on!"

"Oh, no? Just now when I mentioned that Morgan was asking about you, you turned as white as that dress you're wearing and your voice trembled. Why? This isn't the first time I've noticed that happening. We've skated around this issue several times, and I've let you glide away, but not now, not tonight."

"But I've told you all about my experience," she protested. "You know this is my first independent assignment for Your Program Place. I'm not trying to hide anything."

"Aren't you? Information about your experience was only half the question. What about your background? Where are you from? What did you do before you started with that company?"

"None of that matters. I told you, it has nothing to do with my programming ability."

"It does matter, it matters to me. It also matters to my job. Morgan made that very clear this afternoon at our meeting. I rammed this new program idea through over all of his objections. I hired you, so you're *my* responsibility. If anything goes wrong Morgan will have my head and probably my job. Even if he doesn't go as far as firing me he can make life damned unpleasant."

"Fire you?" she gulped. "But that's not fair."

"Since when is life fair? Whitney, it's not just my job I'm concerned about. I'm also concerned about us, about where we're going. When I look at you and touch you, I see the future, a future together. But we can't build a future on deceit."

"I've never lied to you," she cried. When the hot tears gathered behind her lashes she looked down so he couldn't see her pain.

"No, I don't think you've lied, at least not out loud, but silence can be its own falsehood." When she didn't respond his hands came down on her shoulders, forcing her to meet his gaze again. "My God, don't you understand? I opened up my soul for you to see, down by the river front, I gave you everything, yet I got nothing back from you."

"How can you say I gave nothing back to you? I held you in my arms. I welcomed you to my bed."

"We had sex, Whitney. We didn't make love. Damn it, can't you see the difference?" he demanded, his fingers biting into her shoulders. "You don't give of yourself, your soul. Just having your body isn't enough for me. Talk to me. Tell me about yourself. Does our future mean so little to you?"

He was pushing her where she couldn't go! How could she tell him about her past? Saying nothing might threaten their future, but telling him the truth would surely destroy it. The decision made so painfully the night before couldn't be changed. Silence provided her only hope for happiness.

Her hands reached out and gently cupped his face. "How can you doubt that our future means everything to me?" She hesitated, then bared her heart. "I love you, Bradford. You must believe that. Let the past go, please. Isn't love enough?"

For an instant, hearing her declaration of love, he wavered, but then he shook his head. "You say all the right words, but I'm not sure they mean anything. Can there be love without sharing or trusting? I don't think so."

"I can't—"

"I don't want to hear any more excuses. You're hiding something. Tell me what it is. Maybe I can help you."

Urgently needing to feel his comforting arms about her, Whitney wound her arms around his neck then cuddled against him. "You can help me by holding me. That's what I need more than anything right now."

"No!" he snapped, pushing her away. "I'm not going to let you distract me this time. When I hold you I can't think."

"Is that so bad?"

"It is, if it means we don't get anything settled. I want you, Whitney, more than I've ever wanted anyone in my life, and I know you want me—but that's not enough. My experience with Valerie taught me several painful lessons. One of the most important was that passion alone can't sustain a relationship."

The anguish, dulling his eyes to a gray-green, matched her own despair. Desperately she tried to find a way out of the dilemma. "Please try to understand. Someone I loved and trusted very much hurt me deeply. That's why when you told me about your marriage I could empathize with your pain. I'd lived through the same type of disillusionment. Meeting you has given me hope again, but—"

"But you need more time," he finished the sentence for her. "I should have sensed that. You said that first night we went out to dinner that things between us were moving too fast. Apparently they still are. Building trust takes time. Maybe I haven't given you enough of that." He paused, uncertainty making his voice rough. "I guess we could both use a little space to sort things out—if they can be sorted out."

Before she could answer this bleak statement he stood up. "Good-bye, Whitney." Without looking back, he left.

During the next week Whitney descended into her own personal hell. She saw Bradford in the store. On Wednesday she even helped him select one of Mr. Agajanian's Oriental rugs for his apartment. Yet even as they stood together looking at the antique Tabriz hunting carpet they'd chosen and Bradford joked about how he'd like to see her stretched out seductively on its colorful splendor, the things said and not said loomed between them. She felt frozen, helpless to do anything. She hated not telling him the truth. He deserved to know, yet how could she tell him? Each time they parted she felt a little piece of her die.

To avoid the mire of depression threatening to engulf her Whitney hurled herself into her work. Only at her computer could she forget. Only in the safe world of numbers could the hours slip away without pain. Day followed day as she checked and rechecked every loop, every number in the series of subroutines that controlled the weekly inventory report, searching for any mistakes that would account for the one-hundred-and-seventy-five-thousand-dollar discrepancy.

By Thursday the feeling of panic mounted, twisting tighter inside her, as one by one the last subroutines checked out. By one o'clock Whitney felt as if someone had kicked her in the stomach. Damn it, where was the mistake? She'd verified everything she could think of, but obviously she'd overlooked some critical data-entry statement. For a moment she toyed with the idea of calling Your Program Place. She loathed the idea of admitting she needed help, but if she couldn't find the problem she'd have to. Yet her hand didn't reach for the phone.

She sat for a long time, staring at the stack of computer paper. "You're a failure," the column of numbers shouted at her. "You failed with Bradford. You failed with your job." A week ago everything seemed so perfect, now her life lay in shambles. With a sob, Whitney buried her head in her hands, unable to keep the tears away any longer.

Long minutes later a determined sniffle signaled Whitney's victory over her emotions. As she swiped at the tears she muttered bitterly, "Whoever said 'go ahead and cry, it will make you feel better' was an idiot! I feel worse, not better. I bet my face is all blotchy, and the tears made a smeary mess of my printout."

She looked at all the scribbled notes—some smeared, some not—the countless arrows, the columns of figures, and she flipped on the printer. As she watched the printer start spewing out the numbers, she admitted aloud in a resigned voice, "Oh, well, I needed a clean copy to start the rechecking anyway."

Ten minutes later the phone rang. Her "hello" was cut

off. "Miss Wakefield, I want you to come to my office this afternoon."

Hearing the tone of Mr. Greenwald's brusque command, Whitney's already overtaut nerves quivered like the plucked strings of a violin. She swallowed nervously. "Mr. Greenwald, tomorrow we have our regular Friday meeting. Can't it wait until then? I have work here . . ."

"This can't wait," he snapped, interrupting her. "Be here before one. No later!"

The sound of his receiver, slamming into its cradle, barked a message of warning. Dear God, what had gone wrong now? Whitney felt the bile rise in her throat, burning a bitter path into her mouth. The taste of fear; a taste that had become too hauntingly familiar to her during the past two years.

She wasn't going to let Mr. Greenwald's summons do this to her. With an effort she slowed her breathing, willing the sickening feeling to ebb. Why should she jump like a startled rabbit every time the boss called her to his office unexpectedly? It was probably nothing. Maybe he wanted to discuss her next assignment. Maybe another project needed her help. She struggled to form a wan smile. Even better, maybe he was going to give her a raise. Yet even that thought couldn't keep her hands from trembling as she booted down the computer, turned off the printer, then picked up her purse to leave.

The tight uncompromising set to Mr. Greenwald's mouth when she entered his office did nothing to ease her apprehensions. "Mr. Greenwald, I—"

"Why didn't you tell me you were fired from your last job? My God, a bond theft!"

His words hit her like a hammer blow, forcing her words to stumble. "I . . . I didn't tell you because I had nothing to do with that theft. I was innocent, so I thought—"

"I'll tell you what you thought," he interrupted, his ruddy face turning even redder. "You thought I wouldn't give you a job with that on your record. And you were right. I wouldn't have!"

"But if I'm innocent why—"

"Cry innocent all you want to, I don't give a damn," he shouted, bringing his fist crashing down on the desk top. "What I *do* give a damn about are our clients. The thief hasn't been caught. Until that happens you're a suspect! You *could* have done it. That's all our clients will care about."

Whitney opened her mouth to argue, but his hand silenced her as he continued in the same flint-hard voice. "People come to us because we have a reputation for absolute security. You're not a fool, Miss Wakefield. You know that a programmer is privy to the most valuable kind of information; information no client would want to fall into the hands of a thief."

The words "Whatever happened to innocent until proven guilty?" rose in her throat but got no further. What was the use? Being innocent meant nothing to Douglas when he broke their engagement, it meant nothing when Mr. Cramer fired her, and it meant nothing now!

"How did you find out about what happened in San Francisco?"

When she saw Mr. Greenwald shake his head, she insisted, "Don't you think I have a right to know?"

"You've got a hell of a nerve spouting off about rights! What about my right to know about the bond heist before I hired you?"

An angry glint turned Whitney's eyes black. "Look, Mr. Greenwald, someone's trying to sabotage my career. I want to know who!"

"Not a chance! My source is covered, and that's the way he wants it. Why does it matter who told me? The bottom line is—I found out."

As quickly as it had flared, the spark of spirit animating Whitney flickered out. "I guess you're right," she admitted with a resigned sigh. "That *is* the bottom line, and unfortunately for me it isn't going to change."

Her reaction surprised her. No sorrow, no tears, just resignation. Suddenly she realized she wasn't surprised Mr. Greenwald had found out the truth. Nothing had changed. Like a spiteful god, the past refused to let her escape. Somehow deep in her mind, she'd known it wouldn't let go. Maybe that's why she'd been so desperate to succeed at Stanringham's—to have one successful job to her credit before the expected blow fell.

She stood up. At least she could leave with some pride. "You'll have my resignation on your desk tomorrow."

"Damn it, sit down. I'm not finished," Greenwald barked. "You're not going to resign, and I'm not going to fire you, at least not now. If you leave your assignment unexpectedly Stanringham will get suspicious. The man's a security bug. I don't want him digging up the truth and finding out that I sent a suspected felon in on his job. With his connections he'd have the news all over St. Louis in a week." His eyes narrowed. "But don't misunderstand, you're not off the hook, not by a long shot! I'll be watching every move you make. If there's any problem, if *anything* goes wrong, you're out on your butt. You'll never touch a computer again. I'll personally see to that!"

After an hour of aimless driving, Whitney returned to her apartment. She paced through its emptiness as Mr. Greenwald's harsh words replayed. His meaning was menacingly clear—her job, her professional life was on the line. Why was this happening to her again? It wasn't fair! One career shattered, a busted engagement, enough trouble for a lifetime, but she'd refused to let it crush her. No! She'd struggled and put everything together—and now this.

Dear God, what would she do if she lost this job? Whitney rubbed a hand across her eyes, trying to ease away the feeling of despair creeping over her. Taking on the world was a damned lonely business. If she were fired, would she have the courage to start over again? Or, more pragmatically, could she find the money to start over? Every cent she'd saved had gone toward her computer training.

Without thinking, she moved toward the telephone. Her fingers touched the receiver, then jerked away as if jolted by an electrical charge. Tears flooded into her eyes as she stared down at her trembling hand. How long before the need died? How long would it be before the urge to call her parents, an urge she couldn't satisfy, disappeared? All her life, whenever she was troubled, all she'd had to do was reach for the phone. Just her mother's cheery "Hi, Sunshine" or her father's rumbling "How's my kitten?" had the power to shrink any problem.

Now she remembered again the news bulletin—*Killer tornado ravished the Florida coast last night. Details on the hour.* Her parents had only just retired to their oceanside cottage.

Love's Suspect 125

Whitney swallowed down the lump of sorrow threatening to choke her as she heard again in her mind the sound of that endless ringing. Ironically the storm had spared the telephone, but it had left no one to answer her frantic call. She wiped the tears away with the back of her hand. At least they died together; died believing she was happily settled in San Francisco. At least they'd been spared seeing the headlines about the bond theft.

Her nails dug into her palms as she forced her thoughts back to the present. They were gone. They'd never answer her call again. She was alone!

Or was she? What about Bradford? Even as he'd walked out on her he'd made one thing clear: he still wanted her. But could she trust him with her love? She wanted to so desperately that the need throbbed like a raw wound inside her. Yet every time she let that sliver of hope slip into her heart she remembered the love she'd handed Douglas.

Suddenly Whitney's soft mouth hardened into a tight, determined line. Everything else around her might reel with uncertainties, her future might tremble before her, but she had one thing no one could take away—she had herself. She wasn't going to let fate, or bad luck, or whatever was turning her world black, sabotage her again. She would fight for her career. Somehow, some way . . . she *would* succeed. She had to!

She straightened her shoulders. Brave words, but she couldn't very well fight from her apartment, especially when everything she needed was at Stanringham's. So after trying, rather unsuccessfully, to cover up the traces of her tears with makeup, she started for the store.

It was late afternoon by the time she arrived back in the computer room. She didn't waste any time before flipping on the printer, then starting to recheck some figures. Fifteen minutes passed before Eddie's voice carried to her over the rat-a-tat-tat of the printer. "Hey, lady, how's it going?"

Her hands clenched. She willed him to go away, but she knew he wouldn't. Finally with a weary sigh she spun the chair around to face him.

"Have you been crying?" Eddie asked with a concerned frown. "What's wrong? If Mr. Prescott made you cry I'm going to blast him!"

"My gallant hero," Whitney managed a smile. "I can always count on you."

"You sure can! Come on, I'll buy you a cup of coffee and you can tell me about it."

"I really don't—"

"Ah, come on." He grinned eagerly.

When they were settled in the employees' lounge Eddie puffed up his broad chest. "I knew my charm would begin to work on you. See, you've already accepted a date with me. Next stop, the Red Dog Saloon!"

"I hardly think sharing a cup of coffee counts as a date, Eddie."

"There you go crushing my hopes again," he complained, ruffling a hand through his red hair. "But back to your problems. Why were you crying?"

"Would you believe I had an allergy attack?"

"No, I wouldn't. You keep telling me I'm just a kid, but I've lived long enough to know the symptoms. I come in and find those beautiful brown eyes of yours red and puffy, and all week Mr. Prescott has been walking around, snarling at people and looking like a thundercloud. Sounds to me like your little romance has hit a pothole." He raised crossed fingers. "Not that I want to see you cry—but you can't blame me for hoping I may still have a chance."

Whitney had no intention of discussing this topic with Eddie, so she changed the subject. "You make it sound very melodramatic. Actually I think the only thing wrong with me is a large dose of overwork."

"Here's my big chance!" Eddie rubbed his hands together eagerly. "I know just the cure for overwork. Come have a picnic with me Sunday. The leaves are turning, the air is cool, and the chalk bluffs up near Alton are a perfect place to sit and watch the Mississippi flow by. We could—hey, don't start shaking your head no before I've even finished my sales pitch!"

His persistence was endearing, but hopeless. She softened her voice to cushion the rejection. "Eddie, I can't go on a picnic with you."

"Why not? Don't tell me you're working again on Sunday."

No, she wouldn't be working—that she knew for sure. The one thing she needed now was some distance from the program. Maybe getting away from it for a couple of days would give her some fresh insights into where the error might be.

"I'm taking the weekend off. No work, I promise. To be honest, I want to be alone."

His shoulders shrugged. "Okay, whatever the lady says. Get some rest. I'm concerned about you, Whitney. You look exhausted."

Before she could answer, Charlie's cheerful voice boomed from the doorway. "There you are. I might have known you'd be with the prettiest woman in the store." As Charlie lumbered toward their table he commented, "Sorry to break this up, nephew, but the first truckload of Miss Hopper's furs has just pulled in. Looks like we're in for some overtime tonight getting all of them unloaded and up to her department."

"If they shipped an extra mink coat I'll stash it away for you. That should score some points for me!" Eddie winked at her as he shoved back from the table.

"Make it a fox or lynx coat, and you'll score double," she returned his teasing. "Don't let Millicent work you too hard tonight."

"Say, that reminds me of something," Charlie said, stopping at the door. "Miss Hopper asked me to ask you if you'd finished the new program yet, or will her furs have to come in under the old system?"

The last thing Whitney wanted to do was talk about the catastrophe waiting back in her office so she answered vaguely. "Her subroutine is finished, but I haven't had time to integrate it into the rest of the program. Tell her I'm sorry. I know I promised I would try to have it running before the sale, but there are still some problems I have to work out."

Eddie clapped his hands. "Glad to hear you'll be around awhile. I may get you to go stomping with me yet!"

Eddie's uncomplicated adoration acted like a magic elixir to soothe her nerves, allowing Whitney to return to the computer room in a much more positive frame of mind. The printout was finished. As she tore the last sheet from the printer she glanced at the final inventory figure, blinked, then looked again. That couldn't be!

Quickly she grabbed the statement of inventory run under the old system and laid the papers side by side. How could it have happened? She'd made no changes in her program, yet the one-hundred-and-seventy-five-thousand-dollar discrepancy had disappeared! That was impossible—yet the numbers were there, and they didn't lie. The two inventory figures agreed to the penny.

As she stared at the two sets of identical figures the tiny hairs on the back of her neck bristled as if a chill wind had blown across them. She shuddered, confused and strangely apprehensive, then sanity returned. Why was she worried? She should be delighted that the two sets of figures matched. That meant she hadn't made any error in writing the series of subroutines controlling the weekly inventory report. Several plausible reasons for the discrepancy occurred to her. A mechanical failure, a power dropout, or simply a flaw on the disc might have jumbled the numbers. Even static electricity could have caused the malfunction.

Yes, there were a dozen logical explanations, Whitney reassured herself. She was being ridiculous to worry about it! Just because the menacing hand of suspicion had touched her once was no reason to see trouble lurking everywhere. Don't fuss over what caused the discrepancy to disappear, just be glad it wasn't your error, she ordered herself firmly.

Yet she couldn't obey her own order. All the sensible advice in the world couldn't banish the jittery feeling of unease prickling up her spine. The feeling was vague but persistent. There'd been too many coincidences, too many things logic had to explain away, too many accusing looks from Morgan—too many questions from Bradford.

Whitney couldn't see it, and she didn't know where it was coming from, but like an animal who'd been hunted before, she sensed the presence of danger.

Chapter Eleven

THE tangle of sheets and blankets mutely testified that sleep had brought Whitney no peace. Sunday morning she awoke still haunted by the same shadowy premonitions that had bothered her for the past two days. Twice while she was cooking breakfast she caught herself glancing over her shoulder as if expecting to see someone sneaking up behind her. The third time it happened, she turned off the stove, grabbed a sweater, and hurried out of her apartment. She wasn't even sure what she was running from.

As always when troubled, Whitney sought the Mississippi River, hoping to find some tranquillity in its ceaseless flow. The scene was perfect. The water surged below the high bluffs Eddie had mentioned, but for the first time the river failed her. Instead of her emotional turmoil fading, the confusion and fears coiled tighter and tighter within her until the blood pounding in her ears masked the sound of the river.

With effort she forced her breathing to slow to a more normal pace. When some calm returned she drew her knees up, then rested her chin on them as her thoughts moved unhappily on. A new city, a new career, a new man, yet she couldn't escape from that indelible stain of guilt. She felt so guilty—and there was nothing to feel guilty for. She hadn't done anything!

Her head snapped up. Maybe that was the trouble. Maybe she not only felt guilty, she acted guilty. Could Morgan see that? Was that why he'd been poking around in the computer room? Was that why suspicion steeled his gray eyes when he looked at her? Did Bradford sense the same thing? Was that why his questions kept coming?

With a shake of her head Whitney pulled up her thoughts. This treadmill was useless. It went nowhere, solved nothing. Hot tears gathered as she remembered Bradford's words, "if things can be sorted out." Right now she felt she was slowly sinking in quicksand, and she wasn't sure she'd touch bottom before it was too late.

She gazed at the river, wishing the powerful Mississippi flowing past could offer some wise advice, but it couldn't. By the time the setting sun started casting reddish-orange streaks across the water she'd decided that thinking had accomplished only one thing: it had given her a headache! Disgusted, she stood up and started back toward St. Louis.

As she turned the key in the lock of her apartment door she heard the phone ringing inside. Whispering a silent prayer, she grabbed for the receiver. Bradford's "Hello Whitney," answered her entreaty.

"Where have you been? I've been calling for hours."

"Yesterday Eddie suggested we go on a picnic to the bluffs near Alton, and—"

"You mean you've been out all day with him?"

His irritation, crackling over the line, made her smile. "You sound like you care."

"Damn it, Whitney, you know I do! This last week, wanting to be with you but keeping the promise to give you some space, has been torture."

"You're the one who suggested we needed some time apart, not me."

"Everyone should be allowed at least one moment of insanity. Last Saturday night was mine. By this morning I'd decided I'd played the martyr long enough. I tossed and turned, alone and lonely, and decided nothing else mattered except seeing you and holding you. So I called and what happened?" he demanded. "First you're not home, then I discover while I was sitting in my lonesome apartment missing you, you were off cavorting on a picnic with Stanringham's Don Juan!"

"I love to hear that jealous ring to your voice, but I guess I'd better set you straight. Beside your moment of temporary insanity you'd better add a moment of conclusion jumping. I said Eddie *suggested* a picnic. I didn't say I agreed to go with him. Actually I sat alone on that bluff, watching the river and thinking."

"What were you thinking about?"

The thread of husky longing shading his words sent the blood surging through her veins as she admitted, "You, who else? I was thinking about you and about us."

She could almost hear him holding his breath as he asked, "Come to any conclusions?"

"Just one. I'm miserable without you. Did you mean what you said about nothing mattering but being together?"

"Yes."

That one simple word swept away the foreboding cloud that had darkened her week. Whitney's voice sparkled with happiness as she invited, "The brandy's warm and the water in the shower's hot. Why don't you come on over?"

"Let's hope there's no cop between here and your apartment. Although a speeding ticket would be a small penalty to pay to keep that brandy—and anything else—from cooling off before I can get there."

What was, in fact, only a few minutes seemed like hours as Whitney waited for Bradford's knock. Finally it came. Her radiant smile greeted him as she threw open the door. Then Whitney's glance fell to the large parcel he was carrying. "Did you bring me a present? How exciting! It isn't even my birthday."

"Well, you could say this is a present for both of us," Bradford explained, stripping off the brown paper, then unfurling the Oriental rug they'd chosen together.

Whitney's face rivaled the scarlet on the carpet's border as she remembered his delightfully wicked suggestion of how they might "christen" the rug once it lay in his apartment.

"You really do have a thing about the floor, don't you?"

Bradford chuckled at her teasing. "I can't help it. When I see silken splendor like this I just automatically think of you lying against it. You bring out the sheik in me."

"Oh, great!" she commented as he spread the carpet out in front of her fireplace. "You've moved from playing Rhett Butler back to the silent films of Rudolph Valentino. Next thing I know you'll be telling me not to talk."

He raised one rakish eyebrow as he moved toward her.

"Didn't you know one of the first silent films made was entitled *The Kiss*?" His arms swept possessively around her as his lips began brushing silent messages against her mouth. "Who needs words? There are other ways to communicate."

The need to burn away the memory of their time apart made the slow arousing of passion impossible. The instant the warm crevice appeared between her lips his kiss plunged deeper, creating whirlpools of desire that sucked them both into a world where only sensation had reality. His tongue, dipping into the moist valley behind her lips, tasted of her sweetness, then retreated. Whitney moaned at the pleasure lost and followed, feeling the delicious sucking of his mouth as he savored the feel, the velvety texture of her all-giving kiss. Their tongues touched, stroked, until with a gasp Bradford drew away.

His breathing was ragged. "My God, Whitney, I've never known a woman who could kiss me, touch me, and make me explode into a thousand tingling sensations. When I hold you, nothing else in the world matters."

She whispered, "I don't know the words to describe how you make me feel. With you everything is a new experience, totally unique. I've been kissed before, yet each time you touch me it's like the first time."

He sank with the grace of a tawny lion to the Oriental carpet. "Come down here with me, and I'll demonstrate most graphically, most thoroughly, what I feel for you."

A hot, undeniable stab of answering need throbbed through her as she looked at him and saw the raw passion smoldering in his gaze. The power of that one look, so basic, so primeval, reached a part of her never before touched by any man. The wondrous spiral of desire began at the center of her being, then spread out with tendrils of heat until every morsel of her body felt on fire. When Bradford ran a hand up the silky expanse of her calf to the sensitive area behind her knee her desire became so intense Whitney couldn't still a suggestive wiggle of pleasure.

"Come down here," he urged again. "Granted, I'm a leg man, but I'm not satisfied with just your calf."

"Greedy, aren't you?" she teased, savoring the arousing caresses of his fingertips.

"Damn right I am!" he said in a voice thick with need. "I

Love's Suspect

want to nibble on your ankle, stroke over your calf, bite—softly I assure you—the back of your knee, run my hand over the inside of your thigh, taste of your . . ."

His words destroyed the last of her control. Whitney quickly sank beside him, shutting off any more words with her mouth. The demands of their passion drove away everything but need. Buttons ripped and her hose tore as he stripped them down her legs. Her hands showed no caution, either, seeking his bare flesh. Their breathing fell in short harsh gasps as his hands encircled her naked waist. With an infinitely gentle shove he pushed her back until she was lying on the Oriental carpet. It was luxuriantly soft, yet the fire raging within her burned so hotly she didn't even feel the silky nap against her skin. That fire burned higher as his body pressed down against her. It turned every fiber of her being into an inferno, an inferno she knew only the feel of him deep inside her could satisfy.

The stroke of his fingers made her writhe under him until she couldn't stand the torment any longer. With a gasp she pulled him to her, wrapping arms and legs about him, accepting willingly the plunge her body screamed for. The first touch sent a shudder scalding through her, but the ecstasy didn't stop. The rhythm, flesh touching flesh, made the experience more deliciously complete than anything she'd ever known.

Whitney rose eagerly to meet each thrust of his intimate possession, giving in fully, totally to the feelings he stirred. As the crescendo whirled upward one thought shot through her feverish mind: this explosive oneness was what she'd searched a lifetime for. Then another rasp of his tongue, another thrust, drove all but sensations from her mind . . . and every hungry part of her was glad.

Much later he stirred contentedly in her embrace, then raised up on one elbow. Trailing fingers back and forth through the lush pile of the carpet he murmured, "Hmmm, now I feel this rug truly belongs to me. I wonder what else we can find to christen?"

"I thought you were supposed to christen things with champagne."

His gaze traveled slowly down her body, obviously savoring every intimate detail. "When I look at you I get all sorts of creative ideas. Maybe I'll talk Morgan into hiring you as my creative consultant."

At the mention of Morgan's name a frown wrinkled Whitney's forehead. "I doubt if Morgan will want me around any longer than necessary. I keep telling you, he doesn't like me." Then, remembering the papers Morgan had gone through in her office, she added, "And he doesn't trust me."

Bradford's lips, moving over her forehead, smoothed away her troubled look. "That will all change when the new program is finished and running."

"Speaking of my program, you know something really weird happened with the inventory printout I ran Thursday. I ran a second copy, and it didn't agree with—"

His kiss muffled her words. "Whitney, I've held business discussions in some unusual places, but I've never tried to hold one on an antique carpet with a naked woman beneath me, and I don't plan to start now."

His nibbling kisses began making forays into the corners of her mouth, across her chin, then up toward her ear where he murmured, "No more words. Tonight I want to forget about Morgan, computers, anniversary sales, and anything else connected with Stanringham's."

"I'm sorry to drag you into the store so early, but the work on my desk is piled a foot deep," Bradford apologized the next morning as he held open the door for Whitney. "For some reason I wasn't able to concentrate last week."

Millicent's hysterical shriek froze his words. "Help! I've been robbed! Get the police. Call the F.B.I. Somebody help me!"

When Millicent saw Bradford and Whitney running toward her, she cried, "Thank goodness you're here. You've got to do something. My beautiful furs! They were here, and now they're gone!"

"Calm down, Millicent. You're talking so fast I can hardly understand you."

"How can I calm down when a thief has been ransacking my department?"

The word *thief* set a whole collection of butterflies to fluttering in Whitney's stomach. Why did theft follow her like

Love's Suspect 135

an evil specter? Her hands clenched as the all-too-familiar tremor of fear struck.

Bradford's oblique glance caught the trembling, but he didn't pull his attention away from the frantic Millicent. "From the way you were yelling I expected to see empty hangers scattered all over the floor. How can you possibly know you've been robbed? With that consignment from Raphael Designs, there must be a thousand fur coats hanging in here."

"I don't need to find empty hangers to know I've been robbed," Millicent insisted. "You've got to listen to me! Some of the coats I hung Thursday and Friday are *gone.*"

When Bradford tried to protest, she interrupted, "Charlie's over there unloading a dolly. He'll tell you." She raised her voice. "Charlie, come over here."

With a shrug Charlie put down the box and lumbered over to join them.

"Charlie, you helped me hang these coats. Tell Mr. Prescott some of my furs are missing."

"Well now, I'd like to help you, but I'm afraid I can't do that, Miss Hopper. Looks like they're all here to me. But then, Eddie and I carted up so many coats the last couple of days, they sort of all blurred into one big furry blob."

"Millicent," Bradford said sternly, "I think you're stirring up another tempest in a teapot, just as you did about those damned coyote furs, but we'll check it out. We need to hurry, though. I want everything cleared up before the store opens. Go get the packing slips so we can run a quick count."

As Millicent dashed off, he turned to Whitney. "While she's doing that, you go get the printout of the inventory so we can doublecheck."

"That's a good idea, but it will take me about thirty minutes. I'll have to run an update. Since the warehouse only feeds its delivery information in at closing, the printout I ran Friday wouldn't have all the information on it," she explained.

By the time Whitney returned with the printout Morgan had joined Bradford, Millicent, and Charlie. After completing their count, Bradford checked the packing slips, looked at the figures on the inventory statement Whitney had brought, then shook his head. "Millicent, you've had some wild flights of fancy before, but this beats them all. You must have dreamed those coats. According to these, the packing slips, and the inventory count, every last fur coat Raphael Designs shipped is here."

"I don't care what those silly papers say, Mr. Prescott, I *know* some of my coats are gone! I admit I'm no good with paperwork, but I remember furs. Do you see a chevron cut mink or a lynx coat with a sable collar hanging here?" Millicent demanded. "No, of course you don't, because they're not here. Well, they were here Saturday afternoon. And there are others missing, too!"

"Millicent, that's impossible," Bradford argued. "Everything is accounted for. Maybe you're remembering some coats you saw at market, or—"

"No, I'm not! If you would only *listen* to me. I don't care what that obnoxious computer says, but I know furs!"

"But the packing slips agree with the printout. You can't argue with those. Millicent, be reasonable. There aren't . . ."

"I don't like this," Morgan interrupted curtly. "First Amos Snyder loses ten televisions and ten video recorders and now Millicent claims some of her furs are gone."

"Mr. Agajanian didn't have any problem with his merchandise, and those antique carpets are a lot more valuable than television sets," Bradford reminded him.

"I don't care, I want to be sure. Give me the packing slips and that inventory printout. I intend to find some answers!"

When Morgan's glance swung to Whitney, the gray in his eyes glinted like the hardest flint. It took every bit of courage she possessed to meet that look instead of turning and running.

Morgan's voice harshened as he unfairly accused, "We never had this kind of trouble until a few weeks ago. Our security is tight, but still a thief might have infiltrated the store. One thing is damned sure, if we do have a thief it has to be someone on the inside. Don't anyone leave the store. I'll want to talk with each of you later after I've done some checking." After flinging this order at them, Morgan turned and strode off.

"Are you all right, Miss Wakefield?" Charlie asked when the door to Morgan's office had slammed closed.

"You look a mite pale. I know that look Mr. Stanringham threw at you would have curdled cream, but he didn't mean anything by it." He gave her shoulder a comforting pat. "Don't worry your pretty little head about it. The boss has been snapping at everyone lately. He's been working too hard, just like the rest of us. And speaking of work, I guess I'd better finish getting that dolly unloaded before the store opens. I don't want him lighting into me next."

"Oh, dear," Millicent dithered, "we do only have ten minutes before the doors open, and I haven't even given a pep talk to my salesladies. I must tell them to watch for shoplifters. Enough furs are disappearing around here without letting people stuff more into shopping bags."

After she'd hurried off, Whitney attempted to lighten the tense moment. "Millicent does seem to thrive on excitement. Do you suppose that's why she started this robbery nonsense?"

"Forget Millicent. Right now I'm concerned about you. Charlie was right, you do look pale. Care to tell me why the color drains out of your face every time the word *theft* is mentioned?"

Desperately Whitney tried to divert his question. "That has nothing to do with it. As you said, this is probably just another one of Millicent's tempests in a teapot. If I'm pale it's your fault."

"My fault?"

"Sure, I always get shaky if I don't eat breakfast. If you hadn't had such delightfully wicked ideas of what to do instead of eating, I wouldn't have missed breakfast."

Bradford looked at her a long moment, as if deciding whether to question her explanation, then, after an almost imperceptible shake of his head, he held out his arm. "Well, I guess the least I can do is offer to make amends. Miss Wakefield, would you care to join me for some blackberry croissants in the restaurant?"

After breakfast Whitney didn't see Bradford for the rest of the day as she worked on reprogramming the subroutines controlling the printing of the tickets. She had just finished integrating the changes Amos had requested when the telephone rang. The rich baritone of Bradford's voice sent a surge of warmth through her as he said, "What I had in mind for tonight was a romantic candlelight dinner with you—soft music playing in the background, Italian food, and a bottle of perfectly aged Chianti."

"That sounds marvelous. What time will you pick me up?"

"I said that's what I had in mind. I didn't say we were going to get to do it. Next time you see Millicent be sure and thank her for wrecking our evening. That scene this morning set Morgan off on one of his rampages. He's scheduled a meeting tonight at his home with all the executives and buyers to discuss security. Curl up on that Oriental carpet tonight and think of me. Promise?"

She was in no mood to tease as she asked, "Has Morgan found out anything about Millicent's missing coats?"

"You mean the coats she claims are missing," Bradford corrected. "If he has, I haven't heard anything about it. Personally I don't think there is anything to find out. I'm sorry, Whitney, but I've got to run. See you tomorrow."

After dinner Whitney pulled the ticketing subroutines out of her briefcase, unconsciously trying to stifle with work the questions nagging at her, but the questions won. Instead of figures and computer symbols, Millicent's words kept echoing in her mind. *I don't care what that obnoxious computer says, but I know furs.*

Whitney tossed the notes aside and started pacing restlessly across the room. Could some style numbers have been wiped off the computer? If they had been, would she be blamed? Bradford was sure it was just another one of Millicent's scatterbrained mistakes. Yet the uneasy feelings wouldn't rest. She had to know for sure what had happened. But how?

"Ahhh," Whitney sighed in satisfaction as an idea glimmered. Any series of programming steps could usually be formatted in several different ways. She knew those choices were as individual as fingerprints. If someone had broken into her system and made any changes she might be able to spot it. She stopped pacing and frowned. But to do that she needed to scroll through everything she'd entered so far—and as she'd discovered, that could take hours, maybe even days. Wait a minute! It would take hours *unless* she worked when the cash registers in the store weren't competing for the computer time.

Love's Suspect 139

She searched quickly through her briefcase for a telephone number, then dialed. "Charlie, this is Whitney Wakefield. I need to get into Stanringham's this evening to do some checking on my program. Can you fix the alarm system for me?"

"With all this talk about a thief skulking around maybe I'd better come with you."

"Thanks for the offer, but that won't be necessary." She forced a laugh. "As Mr. Prescott said, Millicent just enjoys setting everything in a spin. I'll probably be safer in the store than in my apartment. We've had some break-ins around here, and they're a lot more real than Millicent's imaginary coats."

"Okay, but promise me you'll lock the door behind you. That way you'll be as safe as a newborn babe in her mother's arms."

Despite Charlie's assurances and her brave words Whitney couldn't keep from glancing over her shoulder as she walked through the eerie silence of the store. A few lights had been left on, but still there were a hundred shadowy places where someone could be waiting and watching every step she took. The flesh on the back of her neck prickled as she fought the rising panic urging her to turn around and run back to the safety of her apartment. The click of the lock, closing the computer room door behind her, sounded as welcome as a freighter's whistle to a shipwrecked sailor.

Gradually her overtaut nerves calmed as she scrolled back through her program, searching for any evidence of a deletion or change she herself hadn't made.

Three hours later Whitney turned off the computer, stood up, and stretched. "Well, that certainly was a waste of a good evening! I'd have been better off at home."

The muscles across the back of her neck felt stiff so she started to massage them. Suddenly her hand froze. Was that . . . yes, there it was again: leather brushing against marble. The footsteps came closer. Louder and louder, then silence. Someone was outside the door.

Her terrified glance swept the room. No other door, no place to hide, no weapon. The faint rasp of a key in the lock sent one hand groping frantically for the telephone as the other snatched a letter opener off the desk. She whirled to face the danger as the door crashed open.

"What in hell are you doing here, Whitney? It's after midnight!"

The letter opener clattered to the desk top as she hurled herself into the safety of Bradford's arms. "Thank God it's you! Please hold me, just hold me!"

His arms automatically went around her, but he didn't draw her against him. "You didn't answer my question. What are you doing here?"

When Whitney heard the abrasive edge to his words she struggled out of his embrace. "What do you . . . Well, I could ask you the same question."

"I'm a vice-president of this store. I have a right to be here any time. You don't! I want to know what you're doing here."

"I was working. What do you think?"

"After midnight?" he demanded.

"Yes, after midnight. After the row this morning, I wanted to see if there was a way some fur coats might have been wiped off the inventory list."

"How did you get in? The store's been closed for hours."

"What is this, an interrogation? You sound like a police officer."

"You're damned lucky you aren't talking with the police. If Morgan had found you here you'd be on your way to headquarters right now."

At the mention of the police, Whitney's eyes widened in fear. "Oh, great," Bradford growled, thrusting a hand through his blond hair, "there you go again with the startled deer look. Look, Whitney, stop worrying. I'm not going to call the police, but I do expect to get some answers. How did you get in here?"

"I can't tell you."

"You either tell me or you tell Morgan. Take your choice."

She swallowed, caught between the promise she'd made and Bradford's demands. He waited, but when the silence stretched, he insisted, "We're not leaving until I have the truth."

"If I tell you, will you promise not to inform Morgan? I don't want anyone to get into trouble for helping me."

"Helping you," he repeated. "Ah yes, now the pieces fit. Eddie got a key from Charlie and gave it to you. What did you give him in exchange?"

"How *dare* you!"

Suddenly the anger faded from his expression. "Oh, God, Whitney, I'm sorry. This damned sale, the truckers' strike, the scene this morning—everything's getting to me. I should be thanking you for being so conscientious and instead I'm hurling absurd insults. Is there any evidence someone's tampering with the inventory data?"

Whitney felt a wave of relief surge through her as the suspicious glint faded from his eyes. Her voice sounded confident. "With our code the system here should be secure. Any tampering would have to come through the warehouse, but I can't find even one alteration in my program."

"I guess that settles it. Millicent made the mistake. Come on, I'll take you home. I don't want you driving around St. Louis at this time of night."

As he guided her into his car he commented, "Look, next time let me know when you want to play around in the store after hours, and I'll come and play with you."

His words sounded cheerful, but Whitney didn't miss the whisper of suspicion lurking behind them. And in response her own doubts whispered back, what had he been doing at Stanringham's after midnight?

The question jolted her. She slanted a glance at him out of the corner of her eye. Why had that question popped into her head? She loved him. How could she let even a glimmer of suspicion touch him? Yet that glimmer refused to fade away.

Chapter Twelve

THE next morning Whitney looked at the dark circles beneath her eyes—evidence of another sleepless night—and shook her head. Well, what did she expect? How could anyone sleep with discrepancies popping up then disappearing, coats that could be missing but maybe were not, and footsteps spooky enough at midnight to send her heart pounding. And most people thought programming computers sounded dull!

That thought pulled a weary smile from her as she tucked in the tail of her emerald silk blouse. Then even that weak smile faded. Why didn't she admit it—the strained silence in the car riding home and Bradford's tepid kiss at the door hadn't helped, either. A concealing puff of powder might disguise the dark circles, but no makeup could wipe the traces of unhappiness and uncertainty from her eyes.

A tepid kiss, nothing more. What was happening to them? Until a few days ago Bradford was rapidly becoming the most important thing in her world. And not just because his touch sent a shiver down to her soul. So many small things about him reached out to her; the way his arms had cradled a frightened child in the store until the mother was found, his bravery to risk feeling again after being hurt by Valerie, the crisp snap of his intellect, the way . . .

"Oh, hell, what's the use?" Whitney muttered. Why dream when those dreams might already be slipping away? A witch's cauldron of problems were plaguing them, and she felt helpless to fight back. For a moment her hand hovered over the handles of her briefcase as temptation whispered to call in sick, to escape from the pressure for at least one day. But that wasn't the answer. As her grandmother always used to say, "Problems are like rabbits. If you ignore them they don't disappear, they multiply!" As she headed out of the door Whitney wondered what new problem was going to pop out of the rabbit hutch today.

Late that afternoon Whitney neatly tapped a stack of papers into order, then stretched. "Well, it looks like the rabbit hutch is empty after all. I think I'll celebrate and use that discount Morgan gave me."

She passed by the crowd of shoppers looking through the racks of furs in Millicent's department and walked into the designer area.

The saleslady's offer of help was muffled by the blare of the intercom. "Miss Wakefield, please go to Mr. Stanringham's office. Miss Wakefield, please go . . ."

No smiles greeted her as she walked into Morgan's office. Whitney glanced nervously at Bradford then back at Morgan as he jabbed a finger toward the chair near his desk. The plush Oriental rug under her feet should have cushioned her step in luxury, yet as she hesitantly crossed the room toward the chair he'd indicated she felt like a condemned prisoner taking her last steps.

"All right, Morgan, what is this nonsense?" Bradford demanded. "I was on the phone with Pinkerton's, scheduling the diamond delivery, when Martha interrupted me with your call. Then I rush in here, and you refuse to discuss anything until Whitney arrives."

"Bradford, I know you've been blinded by your personal involvement with Miss Wakefield, but I haven't. I've been doing some checking. Did you know you'd put a thief in charge of redesigning our computer system?"

Whitney's dark eyes squeezed tightly closed against the torrent of emotions pouring over her. Buffeted by fear for her future, angered by the tentacles of the past that wouldn't let go, her heart screamed, Why me? Why me? It was so unjust!

Then, like the tide going out, she felt the storm raging within her begin to wash away as relief replaced the anger. Relief? Yes, that's what she felt. It was over, finally over. Every moment since that meeting with Mr. Greenwald she'd been waiting, half-expecting this blow.

Her eyes snapped open as she sought Bradford's gaze. The look shadowing his green eyes was unreadable, but she didn't care. Even more than being glad the suspense was over, she was relieved the deceit, the evasions were over for them. She'd hated keeping the truth from him, hated having the past rise like a specter between them. She'd wanted to tell him, but fear had frozen the words. Now time had taken that decision out of her hands... and she was glad.

Whitney swung her gaze back to Morgan, meeting his animosity squarely. "Mr. Stanringham, I'm not a thief!"

"That's not what American Securities and the S.E.C. say!" he retorted. "Maybe they didn't have enough proof to arrest you, but you were fired, weren't you? Four million dollars in bearer bonds—what a sweet haul! But obviously it wasn't sweet enough. Your share of the take couldn't have been too generous or you wouldn't still be working." Morgan's gray eyes narrowed to condemning slits. "Or was that one taste of larceny addictive? Did it make you hungry to try it again?"

"Morgan, aren't you jumping to conclusions?" Bradford defended. "Two days have passed, and you still haven't heard anything from Raphael Designs. You know as well as I do that probably means Millicent has made another one of her scatterbrained mistakes."

Morgan refused to back down. "That still doesn't alter the fact that you hired a *thief* to redesign our system. Can you imagine the valuable information she's learned? What if—"

"Please listen," Whitney interrupted. "I admit I was one of the five people who knew about that bond delivery, but I wasn't involved in the theft. When they couldn't find the person who had passed on the information, the S.E.C. made American Securities fire all five of us. How can you brand me with that guilt when I didn't do anything?"

"A very convenient story, but the fact remains—"

"The fact that remains is we're not even sure a theft has occurred here," Bradford reminded him.

"I wouldn't defend her too vigorously," Morgan warned. "You may be joining her in the unemployment line—or worse. Remember what I told you. You hired her. You're responsible for her!"

"Morgan, I know you're concerned about Stanringham's security, especially when millions of dollars in extra inventory is flowing into the store, but I really think you're overreacting to this information. I repeat, nothing has happened." Bradford's tone was soothing, but it failed to calm the other man.

"You're being too cavalier, Prescott. In fact, you don't even act surprised about all this. How long have you known about Miss Wakefield's past?" Morgan held up his hand. "No, don't try to make excuses or lie. Your expression tells me I'm right. Did you know about it when you hired her or did you find out later?"

With the blows coming so fast, Whitney felt like a punch-drunk fighter. She looked in Bradford's face and saw the same thing Morgan had seen. He knew! He knew about the bond theft, the fact she'd been fired . . . everything!

"Bradford, how? Why?" Anguish strangled her words until only a painful whisper escaped. "When did you find out?"

Green ice—that's all she saw when she looked at him. His eyes, that had once blazed with passion, now stared at her with a chill that sent a very different kind of shiver through her. "It doesn't matter when I found out, does it? I waited for you to tell me the truth yourself, but you didn't. That's what matters to me."

"Well, it's not all that matters to me!" Morgan rasped.

Before he could say anything else the phone on his desk buzzed. He yanked up the receiver. "I told you I didn't want to be disturbed for any reason. I don't care who it is. Don't put any calls through!"

The receiver clattered down into its cradle; then there was silence, silence more frightening than accusations. Whitney glanced at Bradford, her eyes desperately pleading with him to find more words of support, but still the silence stretched. Finally she lifted her chin, defiantly deciding the only person she could count on for rescue was herself.

Her brown eyes snapped as she met Morgan's glare. "Mr. Stanringham, I am not going to sit here any longer and let you hurl unfounded accusations at me. You have called me a thief. Do you realize that's slander and actionable? I wouldn't enjoy a messy court fight any more than you would, but I'll call my lawyer if you keep throwing what happened at American Securities in my face." She rose.

Without looking at Bradford, Whitney started toward the door. "Miss Wakefield, come back here," Morgan ordered as her hand touched the doorknob. "I'm not finished talking to you."

"I don't care. I *am* finished talking to you!"

Once outside the door, Whitney's bravado evaporated. Escape! The word drummed over and over in her head, destroying everything but that one desperate need. She didn't even stop in the office to pick up her briefcase as she hurried out of the store toward the safety of her apartment.

An hour later Whitney uncoiled from the sofa and went to splash cold water on her eyes, hoping it would cool the burning left by her tears. Wearily she walked back across the room and picked up the coat she'd discarded. When she opened the closet door and saw the poster of Rhett Butler carrying Scarlett up the sweeping staircase tears again scalded her eyes.

It seemed like years instead of just days ago that she'd bought the poster to give to Bradford. Whitney's fingers twisted into knots, remembering how happy she'd felt that day. How illusory that feeling had been! Bradford hadn't even defended her very vigorously from Morgan's attack. Yet even as her rage churned against him, another part of her couldn't deny her longing for his touch. She slammed the closet door on the poster and the memories.

But her heart knew forgetting him was impossible. The doorbell, shrilling twice, interrupted her unhappy thoughts.

"Whitney, open the door," Bradford demanded, punching the bell again. When she didn't answer he started pounding on the door.

She squeezed her eyes tightly closed, fighting the temptation to let him in. She didn't have the strength to face another scene. What could they say but more angry words? There had already been far too many of those.

The doorbell rang again, followed by more pounding as he insisted, "Come on, Whitney, please open the door. I know you're there. I have to speak to you!"

With a hopeless shrug of her shoulders she turned and walked into her bedroom. Four more rings jangled through the apartment before there was silence.

Dawn was streaking her bedroom with soft shades of rose when Whitney finally fell into an exhausted sleep. It wasn't until the mantel clock bonged eleven that her eyes fluttered open. Her first impulse was to turn over and let sleep claim her again. But reason prodded her to throw back the covers. She hated the idea, but she knew she had to go to the store. If she didn't it would seem like an admission of guilt, and there were already enough suspicions flying around without that.

The gloomy clouds hanging low in a leaden sky matched the grayness of her mood as she pulled open the heavy brass doors. Once in the store the desire to avoid speaking to anyone sent her hurrying through the china and crystal department to the computer room. She turned her key in the lock, but nothing happened.

"I'm afraid that won't work," Eddie interrupted her.

When Whitney turned to face him she saw his embarrassed flush. "I'm sorry, but your key won't fit. Mr. Stanringham ordered me to change the lock first thing this morning."

As Eddie talked, Whitney felt a cold sweat ooze out, covering her forehead in a damp chill. Locked out! Like a recurring nightmare the same terrifying things were happening all over again. She'd been locked out in San Francisco, too. She hadn't even been allowed to go back to her office to get her purse. Instead a policeman had delivered it. Her feeling of being sucked again into the same whirlpool of menace whirled faster when she heard Eddie's next words.

"And he wanted me to stick around here and tell you to go to his office as soon as you arrived." Eddie took a step closer and touched her arm. "Whitney, I'm no good at fancy speeches, but I care what happens to my favorite lady. I know something's up. Mr. Stanringham's face got

Love's Suspect 149

as red as my bandanna when he mentioned your name this morning. Want to tell me what's going on?"

First the locked door, now the order to go to the boss's office—it *was* all happening again! The similarities threatened her, producing a lump of fear that strangled her words.

"Whitney, say something. Are you all right?" Eddie asked, a concerned frown crinkling up his freckled forehead. "You look like you've seen a ghost."

She had. It was a ghost haunting from her past, but she couldn't tell him that. After a nervous swallow she struggled to smile. "It's nice of you to worry about me, Eddie, but I'm all right. I'm just like everybody else. Mention being called to the boss's office, and the butterflies start dancing in the stomach. Believe me, that's the only thing that's wrong."

"Well, you'd better get up there. I've learned from hard experience, waiting never improves Mr. Stanringham's temper."

As soon as his secretary opened his door to admit Whitney, Morgan snapped, "Get Bradford and Millicent in here!"

The only sound breaking the uneasy silence was the irritated tapping of Morgan's fingertips on his desk top. Finally Bradford's knock broke the interminable wait. As soon as they found chairs Morgan exploded, "Millicent, as soon as that consignment of fur coats is returned to Raphael Designs, I don't want you to do any more business with them. It's taken those idiots three days to get me that information I requested!"

Morgan's gaze bored into Whitney. "Unfortunately, they're not the only idiots around. I was a fool not to call and check with International Electric as soon as Amos reported that shortage of televisions and video recorders, but at least now I know the truth. I should have trusted you, Millicent. Your memory for furs was infallible. Thirty-five fur coats are missing, including that lynx with the sable collar and the chevron mink. *Thirty-five!*" he repeated, as his fist crashed down on the stack of packing slips scattered across the top of his desk.

Whitney shuddered as if the blow had hit her, too. Rage coarsened Morgan's voice. "These packing slips are forgeries! They're not the same ones Millicent put on her desk last Saturday afternoon. Packing slips are easy to forge. What I want to know, Miss Wakefield, is how those thirty-five coats got wiped off the computer's inventory."

"Morgan, calm down," Bradford urged. "There has to be a logical explanation for this."

Morgan's glare swung from Whitney to the other man. "There's a logical explanation all right, you just don't want to admit it. I know you two are intimately involved, so you can hardly make an unbiased judgment."

"Mr. Stanringham, I am not a thief. I can't explain about the altered packing slips, but I have an idea what might have happened to the printout. The coats could have been wiped off the computer by a machine malfunction," Whitney said, desperately trying to direct his suspicion away from her. "I have been having trouble getting the new program to run properly. The first time I ran my program there was a huge differential between the inventory figures it quoted and the ones computed under the old system. Then when I reran it a week later the two figures agreed to the penny, and I hadn't made any changes. The only explanation I can think of is that the computer isn't working properly."

Morgan's skeptical frown didn't lift. "And the malfunction just happened to wipe off exactly thirty-five fur coats? That sounds like a very convenient coincidence!"

"Morgan, computers do malfunction. Remember when the machine added a thousand dollars to everyone's bill," Bradford reminded him. "It took us months to straighten out that mess."

Morgan ignored his comment. "Why didn't you mention this malfunction before?" he demanded of Whitney.

"Because I thought it was a flaw in my program. I certainly didn't want to advertise the fact that I had made a colossal mistake."

"Do you have a copy of those programs you ran, Whitney?" Bradford inquired. "I'd like to compare them."

"Sure, they're in the computer room." The angry glitter in her eyes matched Morgan's as she commented, "But I can't get to them since the lock has been changed."

"Who ordered the lock changed?"

"I did, Bradford," Morgan admitted. "You'd hardly expect me to let Miss Wakefield have access to our computers again after I got that call from Raphael Designs, would you?" He tossed a key onto desk. "Go and check those printouts, Bradford, then report back to me."

The strained silence as Whitney walked with Bradford to her office shrieked louder than any indictment he could make. All the premonitions of danger Whitney had been experiencing the last couple of days glowed vividly in her mind. Danger loomed so close it almost became tangible. Her hands trembled when she imagined its presence; lurking like a deadly shadow, patiently waiting to devour her.

Bradford obviously noticed her fear but didn't say anything as he unlocked the door to her office. "The printout is right over there by the—" The words stumbled to a halt as she stared at the empty space where she'd left the printout.

"By the what, Whitney? I don't see anything."

"Don't you understand? It's gone!" she cried, frantically searching through the pile of papers on her desk. "Bradford, believe me, I left it right here." She held up two sets of printouts. "See, the two where the inventory figures agree are here. It's only the one showing the discrepancy that is missing."

The grim set to Bradford's mouth frightened her. "You'd better come with me. Morgan will sure as hell want an explanation for this *coincidence*."

"Let me guess," Morgan observed, reading Bradford's face. "The printout has somehow mysteriously disappeared. What were you trying to do with that story, Miss Wakefield, stall for time?"

"It wasn't a story!" she insisted, fighting back the tears. "I left it in the office and now it's gone!"

Before Morgan could reply the phone rang. "We'll hear the rest of your story in a moment. I think this is the information I've been waiting for."

Morgan's watchful look never left her face as he took the call. "Yes, that's what I was afraid of . . . There's no possibility of mistake, is there? . . . Please make photostats of those records and get me copies as soon as possible. Thank you for checking. Good-bye."

"That was International Electric. They have signed bills

of lading proving they delivered one hundred televisions and video recorders to Stanringham's, so we can add another theft to the list. Another theft, let's don't forget, that also didn't show up on the computer. Thank God we found out about this business before those millions in diamonds arrived. The furs and televisions were probably only the appetizer for the real killing."

Like a fissure suddenly opening beneath her feet, Whitney felt herself falling deeper and deeper into a chasm of trouble. Before she could think of any defense against the charges Morgan was obviously ready to level, Millicent blurted, "Whitney, you seemed like such a nice person. How could you do this to me?"

"Millicent, I keep trying to tell you, I haven't done anything to you or anyone else!"

"Then how come you wanted copies of the Raphael Designs packing slips? You even asked me how merchandise is routed through the warehouse into the store so you could spot the easiest place to nab my coats! You really played me for a half-wit, didn't you? Did you laugh at me when I so eagerly handed you those packing slips?"

"When did this happen?" Morgan demanded curtly.

"Long enough ago to make the forgery a real breeze." Millicent pushed a hand through her already frazzled hair. "I even confessed I didn't check the paperwork too closely. I really made it easy for you, didn't I? What a fool I was!"

Two pairs of accusing eyes challenged her. Bradford looked away. "This is ridiculous," Whitney argued, trying to keep the knot of suspicion from tightening any further about her. "How could I have carried ten televisions out of the store? Don't you think someone would have noticed? Besides, I couldn't even lift them!"

Morgan held up his hand, ticking each damning point off on his fingers. "I know you didn't carry ten televisions out of the store, but maybe you used the same accomplices who helped with the bond robbery. You could easily have manipulated the computer. And you had access to the Raphael Designs packing slips to prepare the forgery."

"I don't believe any of that nonsense!" Bradford protested, finally coming to Whitney's defense. "Everything you've mentioned is circumstantial evidence, and you know it! If you took that to the police they'd laugh at you."

"Maybe and maybe not," Morgan retorted.

"I'd advise you to go slowly, Morgan. I don't think Whitney was kidding yesterday when she threatened to hit Stanringham's with a lawsuit."

"No, I wasn't!"

Morgan's eyes narrowed as his fingers resumed their irritated tapping. "The police can't be kept out of this indefinitely."

"I know they can't. All I'm asking is for a little time," begged Whitney.

"Time to do what?" Morgan countered.

Whitney's chin rose defiantly. There'd been no way she could defend herself against the charges in the bond theft, but she knew every entry she'd made in her program by heart. This time she had a chance to fight against the accusations being hurled at her. She would prove Morgan was wrong. She had to! Her gaze never wavered from his face. "I want time to prove I'm innocent. If someone has broken into my program I know I can find proof."

"And I intend to help her," insisted Bradford, coming to her support. "We'll go through all of Whitney's notes, records, anything dealing with the program she's written. Maybe if we go over it step by step we can spot how the manipulation occurred."

"Until this mess is settled I don't want her anywhere near our computers!"

Whitney winced at his tone. "Mr. Stanringham, that remark is offensive, but since I want this mess cleaned up even more than you do, I won't object. Bradford, I suggest we work at my apartment."

"I'll give you until tomorrow morning, then lawsuit or no lawsuit, I'm calling the police!" Morgan warned.

"If you don't, I will. I want my lovely furs back!" Millicent added as they started out of the room.

Bradford looked around at the reams of computer paper and stacks of flow charts in her office and shook his head. "How in the world did you manage to accumulate this much junk in just a few weeks?"

When he saw his attempt to draw a smile from her had failed, he shrugged. "I'll call Charlie to bring some boxes."

When the older man lumbered into the room and saw their hurried gathering of materials, he grinned. "Glad to see you're finally moving this pretty lady's office. I always said she deserved a classier office than this dump."

"No, we're not moving the office, Charlie. Whitney and I are going to do some work at her apartment this afternoon and need to take these records with us. Did you bring the boxes?"

"Not enough for all this stuff. You folks keep on with your gathering; I'll be back right away with more cartons."

Chapter Thirteen

As THEY started out of Stanringham's a violent clap of thunder rumbled around them, giving warning seconds before the clouds split open to release a torrent of rain. The stack of boxes they carried loaded them down, preventing them from dashing for the car. By the time they tumbled into the automobile's dry interior Whitney was wet to the skin.

Bradford pulled a wisp of dark hair out of her eyes. "I'm sorry. If I had known that downpour was going to hit I'd have given you my raincoat. You're soaked."

His hand slipped under the damp locks to find the nape of her neck. Slowly his fingers rubbed some warmth into the chilled flesh. "But I have to admit I like you like this, my irresistible mermaid. It must be some primeval instinct stirring within me when I see you dripping wet."

Troubled brown eyes met his. "I don't know where the next blow will come from, Bradford. I'm . . . I'm . . ." the words stumbled to a halt.

"You don't need to say it. You're afraid. Whitney, I'm here for you, believe that. And I'm trying to help, but I can't unless you tell me the truth."

"I am telling the truth!" she snapped. "Damn it, I just wish someone would believe me! Even you act like—oh, forget it." She pulled away from his touch.

His gaze locked with hers for a long moment. "I want to believe you—God, how I want to believe you!" Then without waiting for her reply he started the engine.

Once in her apartment Bradford's glance raked over her body, then he shook his head. "I hate to say this, but as much as I enjoy the way that wet blouse clings to your luscious curves, I think you should go change. You don't need a case of pneumonia on top of everything else."

"I won't be long," she replied, carefully matching his neutral tone. "Why don't you start some coffee while I change into something dry."

She was rubbing a towel briskly through her hair when she thought she heard the front door snap closed. With a confused frown she poked her head around the corner. "Bradford, did you forget something?" When he didn't answer she raised her voice and called. "Bradford, are you there?" Again she heard nothing.

He must have gone to get something in the car, she decided as she stepped out of her wet skirt. Before she could think about it any more a shiver rippled over her damp skin, raising goosebumps and making her forget everything but the desire to bundle up in something warm.

The coffee pot gave its last aromatic thump as she reentered the living room. Bradford glanced up from the flow charts he was studying. "How about getting us some coffee? Then I have a couple of questions about how you operated on the data for these subroutines."

For hours they went over and over the program step by step. Finally, Bradford leaned back. "So far everything checks. I didn't spot any area where data manipulation could have occurred, did you?"

"No, I wish I could say I did! But if someone's been tweaking with my program I'm going to find out!" she vowed.

He glanced at his watch. "Do you realize we've been working almost four hours? I'm starved. How about some dinner? Then we'll take another run at it."

"I could fix something here. I've got stuff for spaghetti sauce in the refrigerator."

He stood up then reached to help her arise. "I had in mind some Italian food, but not here. How about going to the little restaurant where we shared our first dinner? I think it would do us both good to take a break and forget about computers, Stanringham's, and . . ." he paused then reluctantly added, "and missing fur coats. You'll need your raincoat. It's still pouring out there. Maybe instead of searching through these printouts we'd be better off starting an ark," he joked, trying to coax a smile.

Love's Suspect   157

Before she could anticipate what he planned to do, he'd walked to the closet. "I forgot my umbrella. We'll have to use yours."

Suddenly, remembering the poster she'd hidden, she rushed toward him. "Bradford, no! Don't open that door!"

Her plea came too late as the door swung open. For a stunned moment, he stared into the closet. When he turned to look at her, the rage darkening his expression made her stumble.

"Bradford, what is it? You look—"

"Shut up, Whitney! I've heard enough, *more* than enough!"

With icy control more frightening than any shouted words he reached into the closet. Slowly his hand reemerged holding a lynx coat with a sable collar. Her eyes flew to the hang tag boldly emblazoned *Raphael Designs*.

"How did that—?"

"Damn it, stop the innocent act! Morgan was right. You've tricked us all. Me most of all."

"You've got to listen to me! I've never seen that coat before!"

He didn't appear to even hear her as the angry words continued. "After Valerie, I thought I knew every filthy trick a woman could pull to get what she wanted. I was wrong. You told me you had expensive tastes, I just never believed you'd shaft me to satisfy them. Was inviting me back to your apartment all part of the plan? Did you think sleeping with me would lull my suspicions?"

Tears blinded her eyes as his fury washed over her. She stretched out her hands to him, pleading with him to understand. "How can you ask that? Do you think my kisses could lie?"

He refused to listen. "From the first moment I saw you my instincts said you were my hope, my future. How could they have been so wrong?"

"Bradford, I felt the same way. I looked up into those smoky-green eyes of yours and saw . . ."

"Saw what, a patsy?" he demanded harshly. "Is that what you saw? Oh, you can be proud of your performance. You made a fool of everyone. Even after I knew about your past, I wouldn't listen to Morgan's suspicions. Even when you didn't have an alibi for the Sunday when the furs were stolen I didn't doubt you. Hell, I even put my job on the line for you!" he raged, throwing the coat at her.

As she stared at the damning coat lying at her feet, a terrifying feeling of déjà vu gripped her. It was all happening again: the suspicions weaving around her like a lethal cocoon, being innocent yet unable to prove it, accusations she couldn't refute.

I'm not guilty! Why won't anyone believe me! her thoughts screamed.

Then out of that terror a flash of horrifying insight seared into her mind. She'd been so busy diverting suspicion from herself she hadn't stopped to think, *If I'm not guilty, someone else is.* And like the last piece of a puzzle falling into place, she finally saw the truth.

She picked the coat up and hurled it back at him. "Here, this is yours, not mine. I heard you go out and then come back. Is that when you put it in the closet so you could conveniently find it later? I guess after the haul you've made using one fur coat as planted evidence is a small price."

"That nonsense won't fly, Whitney. I've heard enough of your lies."

"Lies? How *dare* you accuse me of lying? You set me up as the convenient suspect, didn't you? You hired me. You knew my past would make me the logical suspect. You know as much about programming as I do. You even admitted you need money. And you had a key to the store and to the computer room!"

"You were the one I found there at midnight!"

"Yes—and what were you going there? You never explained that." Her brown eyes glittered like the hardest obsidian. "Why didn't you mention my key to Morgan this afternoon? Were you keeping it as the last bit of incriminating information, the final *coup de grace* that would finish me off?"

"No, I thought I was protecting you. Me protecting you, isn't that the ultimate farce?"

"Farce. How apt for you to choose a theatrical word. God, it really is funny!" Her mocking laughter rose hysterically. "You always said you wanted to be an actor. What a magnificent performance! With that sob story about your marriage, you even maneuvered *me* into inviting *you* back to my apartment. How did you keep from laughing?"

"You're clever, Whitney, I'll have to admit that," he growled, his anger rising again to match hers. "But turning all the suspicion back on me isn't going to work. You can't escape from this one as you apparently did in San Francisco." He kicked at the fur beneath his feet. "This coat nails you cold."

Blindly she struck back. "Go ahead and call the police. But when you do, be prepared to explain why you pushed Stanringham's into redoing the program just when millions of dollars of extra merchandise was flowing into the store. In all that confusion the theft should have been easy. And don't forget, no one else has had access to my apartment but you to plant that damned coat." Her tone slashed at him as she slammed home the last damning point. "And besides Morgan Stanringham, no one else could have gained access to the program but you. You were the only other person who knew the code!"

If she hadn't been so angry the bitterly disillusioned twist to his mouth might have touched her heart. Instead she marched to the phone and yanked up the receiver. "Go ahead. What are you waiting for? Call the police!"

Without looking at her, Bradford stepped over the coat and headed for the door. As his hand turned the knob she heard him mutter, "And I was fool enough to fall in love with you." Before she could react he was gone.

Hour after hour Whitney huddled in misery on the sofa as piece after piece of evidence piled up against Bradford. Tears fell, then dried, then fell again as she tried to argue against the damning logic . . . and failed. It couldn't be anyone else. But would anyone believe her? Did she want anyone else to believe her? Even to save herself could she condemn Bradford?

Whitney buried her head in her hands. Hot tears trickled through her fingers as she asked herself over and over how she could have fallen in love with such a man. She'd thought she loved Douglas, but Bradford had reached feelings much deeper. He touched so many chords within her. How, how could she have been so wrong?

Suddenly her head snapped up as a new idea struck. What if the powerful seeds of her love weren't wrong? What if that love knew instinctively what rational thought ignored? If Bradford wasn't the thief, then . . .

A dozen vignettes flashed through her mind. This time no doubts clouded her certainty. How could she have been so blind? Everything fit. How could she have suspected anyone else?

Without waiting to put on her raincoat she hurried out into the night. The rain had let up to a drizzle as she drove rapidly through the deserted streets toward Bradford's apartment. When he answered her frantic knocks he had on his raincoat. He looked stunned. "Whitney, what are you doing here? I was just coming to you."

He grabbed her hand as if afraid if he let go she'd disappear, then pulled her into his apartment. Once inside his arms swept about her. "Can you forgive me for what I said, for all the awful accusations I threw at you? I don't know who's responsible for the robbery. I only know one thing: I love you! And that love's not wrong—it can't be!" he vowed savagely.

Tenderly Whitney drew away just far enough so she could see up into his face. "They say love is blind. I think we both need Seeing Eye dogs. The truth's been in front of our faces all the time, but neither of us stopped distrusting long enough to search for it. When I admitted to myself nothing mattered but my love for you, the blinders came off. I know who stole the furs and the televisions. I know how, and I have a plan."

For the next thirty minutes he didn't say anything as she outlined every incriminating bit of evidence and her plan to catch the thief in the act.

He looked almost sad when she finally finished talking. "It's hard to believe, but it makes such perfect sense that it has to be the answer."

"Do you think my trap will work?"

"It has to. No one with sticky fingers could possibly resist such a setup. But there is nothing we can do about it until tomorrow."

"I know," she murmured, nestling contentedly in his arms. It felt so right, so natural, as if she'd at last come home. "I guess we'll just have to think of some way to while away the hours until the morning. Any ideas?"

Strong fingers tilted her chin up, but before his kiss could blot out everything else she laid a finger across his lips. "There have been enough misunderstandings be-

Love's Suspect

tween us to last a lifetime. But I don't want anything marring the happiness I feel right now, so I have to ask this. When did you find out about that bond theft in San Francisco?"

He rested his cheek against her dark hair as he talked. "I knew from that first day in my office that there was some darkness shadowing your life. Seeing the expression in your eyes when you looked at your Porsche made me even more sure. I waited, I wanted you to come to me, to tell me about that pain from your past, but you wouldn't. After that blowup the night of our Greek dinner I decided I had to know what it was if we were ever going to have a future together. It only took a few phone calls to find out the truth. I wish you could have trusted me."

"I wanted to tell you, but fear has a way of corroding faith." She twisted around in his arms so she could look into his eyes. "Handing me back that faith is the greatest gift your love has given me. Since San Francisco, fear has been like a ghost, haunting my every breath, making me vulnerable. But driving over here, I suddenly realized for the first time in two years I was free of it."

She twined her arms around his neck. "I wonder if I can think of some way to thank you for that precious gift?"

He chuckled his best wicked chuckle. "Oh, you're going to thank me, all right, in several delightful ways I can think of, but not before I ask you a question. What was in that closet you didn't want me to see?"

When she told him about the *Gone with the Wind* poster his gaze flickered to his staircase. In one powerful motion he swept her up into his arms and started across the room. "This may not be Tara, but I can assure you of one thing. The bed up there is just as seductively inviting as the one Miss Scarlett found at the top of her staircase!"

Chapter Fourteen

EARLY the next morning, Whitney stirred lazily in Bradford's arms. "Come back here," he ordered sleepily, tightening his embrace around her until her body nestled intimately against his again. "I'm not going to let you go anywhere."

"I'm surprised you have any energy left to hold me," she teased, letting a contented sigh escape.

His hand moved in a loving sweep over the curve of her shoulder to the cushioned softness of one breast. "Now that you mention it, remind me to scold you for keeping me awake all night."

"I didn't hear any objections at the time."

He gave her nipple a playful tweak. "I'm too much of a gentleman not to give a lady what she asks for."

"*Asks* for?" Whitney repeated, pretending indignation. "I don't remember asking for anything last night."

Bradford shifted her in his arms until his lips found the pulse throbbing in her throat. Between tender nibbles he murmured, "I keep telling you, Whitney, there are other ways to communicate besides using words. You may not have said anything, but you made it very clear what you wanted . . . and wanted . . . and wanted . . ."

As his kiss began stirring the embers of desire, Whitney squirmed suggestively against him. "See what I mean?" he whispered. "Just then you didn't say a word. Still, I know exactly what's going on in your mind. Isn't learning body language fascinating?"

"It sure is," she agreed, wrapping her arms around him. "I wish the lesson could continue all day, but it can't."

"Why did you have to remind me of the world outside your embrace?" he groaned.

"Because the trouble won't go away by ignoring it."

"I wish it would, but I know that's impossible."

"Bradford, I'm trying not to be vindictive, but someone set me up. I can't forget I was supposed to take the fall for the thefts. I might even have ended up in prison! I want this mess cleared up, now. You know we can't go on with our lives until it's settled."

He propped himself on one elbow so he could look down at her. "There's one thing I want settled right now, Whitney! Any going on with our lives is going to be done together. Walking out on you last night was the worst thing I've ever done. We're not going to be apart like that ever again. Understand?"

"Ah, so masterful!"

"Yeah, real masterful!" he muttered in disgust. "So masterful I suspected the woman I love of being a thief while the real culprit was operating right under my nose."

"You didn't have all the pieces; I did," she soothed, reaching up to smooth the troubled frown from his forehead.

"That's what I plan to tell Morgan. I want him to know who's responsible for finally seeing the truth." Reluctantly he rolled away from her. "I'm afraid any more lecherous designs on your enticing body are going to have to wait. I want to catch Morgan before he leaves for the store. It's going to be one hell of a day!"

Whitney could hear Morgan's doubting words crackling through the receiver as Bradford told him her reconstruction of the thefts. When Bradford finished explaining, he said, "I know we still don't have any hard evidence, but you have to believe her. It's the only explanation that makes sense. At least give Whitney a chance to prove she's innocent. She has devised a plan to trap the real thief. I'll give the phone to her so she can tell you about it."

Bradford put his hand over the receiver. "He's not totally convinced yet. Remember, we're dealing with some longtime loyalty here, but he has agreed to listen to your plan."

Whitney shut her eyes tightly, gathering her courage, then reached for the receiver. "Mr. Stanringham, I know you don't want to believe my explanation, but it has to be

Love's Suspect

correct. With luck, the plan I've devised will catch the thief red-handed. It's a two-step idea," she explained. "First we let the thief think the conspiracy to have me take the fall for the robberies has succeeded; then we offer such a tempting target he won't be able to resist using his scheme one last time."

"Let me hear the details."

Fifteen minutes later Morgan conceded, "All right, I admit it's a brilliant idea. If you're right, it can't fail. But I warn you, if you're wrong, nothing is going to save you!"

"If you make those phone calls I suggested you should be convinced."

"We'll see," he answered with obvious skepticism. "Let me go over this one more time. Bradford's coming into the store as usual this morning, but I won't see you until one this afternoon at the cosmetic counter. Right?"

"Yes, I'll be waiting there, trying to look as guilty as possible. Good-bye."

After Whitney hung up the phone, Bradford gathered her in his arms. "This will be my greatest acting job yet. I will have to give the performance of my life to keep my love for you from showing!"

She wound her arms about his neck and raised her lips to his. "Why don't you give me a demonstration of your feelings now? Maybe that will get it out of your system before you have to go to work."

"I'll never get you out of my system," he murmured against her lips.

Four hours later Whitney stopped at the cosmetic counter. Turning her back to the escalator, she reached for a tester of perfume. As she sprayed a sample on her wrist she caught a glimpse of her watch, then tensed, waiting.

"There she is!" Right on cue, Morgan's voice sliced through the stillness of the store.

Pretending to be startled, Whitney jumped, then whirled to face him. When she saw Morgan, Bradford, and the two policemen stalking toward her she let the tester slip from her fingers. It splintered on the marble floor, spewing glass and expensive scent everywhere. As planned, the noise attracted attention—especially the attention of the one person for whom the scene was being staged.

A thunderous scowl darkened Bradford's face as he reached her side. "I'm sorry, Whitney. I didn't have any choice. I had to tell the police about the stolen fur coat I found in your apartment."

One of the burly officers grabbed her arm. "Miss Wakefield, Miss Whitney Wakefield?" he demanded.

When she nodded, he continued, "Miss Wakefield, we have a warrant for your arrest. You have the right to remain silent. If you give up that right . . ."

The familiar formula droned on in front of the fascinated crowd of shoppers. When he finished, she cried, "But I didn't do anything! Bradford, you must believe me! Please help me."

His voice snapped with icy efficiency. "I'll call a lawyer for you, that's all. What else can you expect, since you made a fool of me along with everyone else?"

"Get her out of here, officers," Morgan ordered. As they marched her away, he turned to Bradford. "Thank goodness we caught the thief before all those diamonds arrive tomorrow."

The police car delivered her to Bradford's apartment, and the waiting began. The hours crawled until Bradford arrived. After his welcoming kiss, he murmured, "This is the first night of a lifetime of coming home and finding you waiting for me. Let's celebrate."

"We can't. You know I don't dare go out of this apartment. If someone saw me it could ruin all our plans. I couldn't even go get groceries to cook you dinner, and since you have the typical bare bachelor's pantry we may starve."

"Not when there's a carry-out Chinese food place on the corner. You uncork the wine and lay out the chopsticks; I'll be right back."

Soon the savory smell of moo goo gai pan, wafting out of the carton, filled the room while Whitney complained, "I thought the pressure of being a suspect was nerve-racking, but this waiting is worse. The minutes drag like hours."

"I hate to see you bored. Ah, I know." He leaned over and whispered suggestively in her ear. "How about a nice long hot shower, then a massage? I'll bet that would take your mind off the waiting."

Bradford's suggestion worked marvelously. Whitney

didn't think about the theft or the trap they were going to lay until the next morning.

When he was ready to leave for Stanringham's, Whitney noticed the excited sparkle turning his green eyes to emerald and laughed. "You're really enjoying this, aren't you?"

He paused with his hand on the doorknob. "I could insist that I'm merely doing what every citizen should do, combat crime, but you're right. Somehow it doesn't seem right to be enjoying this, but I am. Deep inside I must have a yen to play James Bond as well as Rhett Butler. All this skulduggery is exciting. Besides, I have a personal score to settle. Someone is not only stealing from the store, but they made a fool of me and tried to harm you. I want that person viewing life from behind bars! We'd better synchronize watches. Your call needs to come exactly at eleven."

At a quarter of eleven Bradford sent his secretary away on an errand. After opening his door a crack he placed a phone call of his own. Ten minutes later he heard the sound in the outer office he'd been waiting for. He smiled to himself. All the players were in place. When Whitney's call rang through he grabbed the receiver and began the monologue they'd carefully rehearsed.

"Hello, Joe. How's the president of Windsor Diamonds? . . . Your diamonds arrived a few minutes ago and are in the safe. Yes, the floppy disc with the inventory count was with them. As I understand it, that's the only copy we're getting. Is that correct?"

Bradford let loose a peal of laughter. "I knew you'd computerize yourself into trouble someday. Did the power drop wipe everything off your computer? . . . What tough luck. That means that disc you sent is the only record of the diamond shipment there is, doesn't it? . . . I'm glad this didn't happen a few days ago. We've had a thief manipulating our computers, but she's been arrested. I'm glad she didn't have a chance to steal a handful of those diamonds and then alter the disc. With your copy gone there would be absolutely no way to trace the loss. I'd better put that disc in the safe with the jewelry. . . . I don't blame you for being nervous. You sent over a million dollars in jewelry and loose stones to us. . . . Of course. I'd be happy to meet your representative here before the store opens Monday morning so we can physically inventory the shipment together and get a hard copy of the list to you."

After Bradford hung up the phone, he saw a movement outside his door. Someone had been listening to his conversation. For one brief moment he allowed the satisfaction of knowing the noose was slowly tightening to show in his smile, then he reached for the telephone again. "Morgan, we've got another problem. The president of Windsor Diamonds just called. They're having more trouble with computers than we are. He said . . ."

Early Sunday morning, after hiding their cars a dozen figures moved silently through Stanringham's to their assigned places. Hidden in dressing rooms and behind office doors the police, Morgan, Bradford, and Whitney waited. Hour after hour they strained to hear the anticipated sounds, but nothing broke the frustrating silence. With each sweep of the minute hand Whitney's agonizing doubt grew. She had no proof, just suppositions. What if she were wrong? Bradford must have seen the uncertainty dulling her eyes, because he moved quietly across the dressing room to put a reassuring arm across her shoulders.

He leaned toward her ear to whisper something, then froze. Whitney held her breath. Was that—Yes, that time she'd definitely heard the sound of someone walking down the marble aisle!

The footsteps stopped. A few moments later they heard the squeak of a hinge needing oil. "That's the safe door," Bradford whispered. Still neither of them moved from their hiding place.

Ten minutes later they heard the footsteps moving away, then more silence. "The police said to wait five minutes, then follow," he whispered. "They want to catch the thief in the act of actually altering the inventory on the disc."

Relief mixed with regret inside Whitney during that agonizing five-minute wait. The thief had come. No guilt would shadow her days again. Yet, at the same time, being responsible for sending someone to prison was sobering. Especially when . . . A soft tap on the door pulled her out of the useless musing.

The police captain opened their door. "Come on. Follow me, but keep quiet!"

They moved stealthily toward the computer room. Whitney swallowed when she saw the patrolmen draw their guns. The officers motioned everyone back, then charged into the room, guns leveled. Through the open door Whitney saw what she expected, disappointing the tiny part of her that hoped it wouldn't be true.

Eddie looked up, the color draining suddenly from his face. "Ah shit!" he snarled, smashing his fist down on the computer keyboard.

"Damn it," Charlie whined, "I tried to tell you I smelled a trap! But would you listen? Hell no! You and your cocksure plan that couldn't fail!"

As the police snapped handcuffs on them, Eddie's glance met Whitney's, and he grinned sardonically. "Think of me sometimes foxy lady. Believe it or not, I'm sorry you ended up being our patsy. We didn't have any choice. You were the most convenient suspect around."

After the police had left with their prisoners, Morgan took Whitney's arm. "I think we've all earned a drink. Why don't you go up to my office? I've got a phone call to make, then I'll join you and we can drink a toast to the success of your trap. And if you don't mind, you can also answer some questions, Whitney. I still don't have all the details about how Eddie and Charlie pulled off these robberies."

Once he joined them in the office Morgan said, "Before you say anything, Whitney, I want to offer you my profound apologies. My inaccurate suspicions must have turned these last few days into a nightmare for you."

"They did, I won't lie about that, but it's over now."

"Over except for your explanation," Morgan reminded, pouring the wine. After giving each of them a glass he lifted his to Whitney. "A toast first to your insight and my instincts. Before you launch into that explanation I have one of my own. I believe *paranoid* is the word Bradford tossed around for the way I acted toward you, but I had a reason. I want you to understand that. Any good retailer lives by his instincts; instinct to know which designer will be hot next season, instinct to know when to time promotions, and a hundred more. Over the years I've learned to trust my instincts."

"And those instincts flashed a red alert as the anniversary sale neared, right?"

"Perceptive as always," Morgan nodded in tribute to her. "I expected trouble. Theft is always a problem in a department store, but I realized the confusion of the sale provided the perfect cover, not just for the usual pilferage, but a major loss. You were the stranger, so those suspicions were aimed at you."

"Is that why you were in the computer room that morning?" she asked.

"Yes. Stupid, wasn't it? I have no idea what I expected to find," he admitted ruefully. "I don't know a thing about computers! I should have looked closer to home. Charlie! Even after seeing him marched out of here in handcuffs it's still hard to believe. He's been with Stanringham's for years!"

"That's the principal reason they almost succeeded," Bradford observed. "You trusted him. It wouldn't surprise me to learn Charlie had been helping himself to small items for a long time, but I think Eddie was the one who saw the possibilities for a big haul."

"Yes, I'm sure you're right," Whitney agreed. "Eddie likes the good life. He drives an expensive car, enjoys taking his dates to the best places—and all that's hard to do on a dock worker's pay. Plus, from a couple of things he said, I think underneath that cheerful facade there's a lot of anger against authority. Remember when he made that crack about how the officers and the top brass always get the girl?"

"Okay, so much for the psychology. Now I want the details. Oh, one last thing before you start. The call came through last night. Your guess was right. Eddie did learn computer programming in the navy."

Whitney nodded. "That's why he thought of using the computer to conceal the theft. He knows about computer mentality. People believe what computers tell them. With those television sets, when the computer said ninety, the count agreed, so it never occurred to anyone to ask if the data base had been manipulated. He depended on the probability that no one would take the trouble to check back through all the paperwork. It was almost the perfect crime."

"Perfect, except for Millicent's memory of furs!"

"There were other things that should have tripped them up. The other night, when the pieces finally fell into place, I saw a lot of clues I shouldn't have missed," Whitney confessed. "I should have suspected something was wrong on Halloween. That afternoon I tried to work through the modem. For a while everything was fine, but then the data flow slowed. I blamed it on overloaded telephone lines. I realize now the data input-output slowed down because two people were working on the same system. Eddie was in the store wiping inventory they'd stolen off the computer at the same time I was trying to feed in my entries. You told me that first day that Charlie had keys to everything. It was easy for them to come and go at will."

"I should have thought of that, but I didn't. What finally made all the pieces fall into place for you?" Bradford asked. "After I left you I sat for hours trying to sort out the charges and countercharges we'd hurled at each other. I knew *I* hadn't done it, and God knows I didn't want to believe *you* had. But everything fit so perfectly I couldn't see any other answer."

"I couldn't, either, for a long time. Only the three of us knew the code, so I kept asking myself how anyone else could have broken into my program. My mind had no answer for that." Whitney's gaze melted tenderly into Bradford's as she murmured, "But my heart saw the truth. I loved you, and I wouldn't have fallen in love with a thief!" Her loving smile drew him like a magnet, pulling him to her side.

Morgan let the kiss go on for several seconds, then interrupted, "Oh, for heaven's sake, will you two please save all this billing and cooing for later! Let's get back to the code. How did Eddie break it?"

Whitney paused as she struggled to draw her delightfully wandering thoughts back to the crime. "As you know we decided to use my birthday, March seventeenth, for the code. That evening after our fight I kept coming back to one thing: Bradford and you were the only other people who knew the code. But any code can be broken, especially one as simple as that. Once that fact dawned on me a scene popped into my head and everything snapped into place."

"I'll bet it was a scene with Eddie. Every time I turned around he was underfoot," Bradford complained.

"Yes, he did seem most enamored with you," Morgan agreed.

"That's what he wanted everyone to think, including me, and it worked. Actually his Don Juan act was part of a very clever plan. Every time he brought me doughnuts or asked me out on a date he learned more about my progress, my work schedule, even the type of computer language I was using. But back to the code." Again Whitney's eyes sought Bradford's. "The afternoon before our Greek dinner, Eddie saw me writing a check for that white gown. When I handed my driver's license to the clerk he grabbed it, pretending to admire the picture. My birthday's on there. He knew there was no reason for us to use a complicated code, so he tried that date and obviously it worked."

"You're right. It was after that weekend that you discovered the discrepancy had disappeared, wasn't it?"

She nodded. "It would have been a snap. Once Eddie had the code he could break into my program and adjust the data base so both inventory figures agreed. Again, instead of being suspicious, I blamed it on a malfunction. By the time Millicent insisted some furs had been stolen, Eddie or Charlie had had time to steal the printout showing the discrepancy, and I had no proof, except my word, that it had ever existed."

"You can see why you looked so suspicious, especially after I found that fur coat in your closet," Bradford commented. "How in the world did they ever get into your apartment to plant it? Surely they didn't risk asking the manager to unlock your door."

"They didn't have to. Eddie had a key."

"Why would you give him a key to your apartment?" Bradford demanded, a hint of jealousy shading his voice.

"I didn't. They had me set up as the suspect from the first. Eddie was stationed in San Francisco at the time of the bond robbery. When he met me he must have remembered I was a suspect in that case and decided I was the perfect foil for their plan. On that Friday you were in Dallas, Eddie offered to carry the portable computer out to my car. When we got there we discovered it had a flat."

As her thoughts ranged back over that afternoon she suddenly remembered meeting Charlie walking back into the store as they left. Her eyes narrowed. "In fact, I wouldn't be surprised if Charlie let the air out of my tire so Eddie could offer to take me home. It's called casing the joint, I think. Anyway so much happened after that, I forgot Eddie had installed a new dead bolt lock on my door. Getting a duplicate key made would have been easy."

"We really played into their hands, didn't we? We even called Charlie for those boxes, so he knew we were going to be working in your apartment."

"When he left to get those boxes he probably told Eddie to plant the coat. They had a lot of luck. They had no way of knowing you'd open that closet, but the long shot paid off."

Bradford winced, obviously remembering their bitter quarrel. "They not only manipulated the computer, they manipulated us around just like pieces on a chessboard. Charlie even called me at midnight, telling me the alarm had been tripped. He knew I'd investigate and discover you working late. They really played me for a fool!"

"Don't feel bad," Morgan commiserated, "they pulled my strings too. How do you think I learned about the bond theft? Eddie casually mentioned that the name Whitney Wakefield sounded familiar. Then, as if the memory had suddenly struck him, he put your name with the bond robbery. My suspicions did the rest, I'm afraid." Morgan shook his head. "Almost everything fits. There is just one piece missing. I'm still confused about the pattern of the crime. After we found the appliance shortage I admit I was lulled when nothing happened the next week. Those Oriental rugs are a lot more valuable than televisions."

"Their value rests with their uniqueness," she reminded him. "I'm certainly not an expert, but I imagine one-of-a-kind antique carpets would be difficult to fence."

"Whitney, on my way into the office I called Mr. Greenwald," Morgan said. "I knew all of this would be hitting the newspapers and wanted to make it crystal clear to him that you were not involved. That, in fact, you were responsible for catching the thief. He sounded so relieved I got suspicious. Finally he confessed he already knew about the bond theft."

"How? That's the one loose thread I couldn't tie up."

"American Securities is opening an office here and needed a computer system designed," Morgan explained. "When Mr. Cramer contacted Your Program Place he—"

"He hit the ceiling when he discovered I might be working on the system," interrupted Whitney. "Right?"

"Yes. Mr. Greenwald sends his congratulations and, by the way, his apologies."

"Apologies? For what?"

"For suspecting you of complicity in the bond theft. Mr. Cramer called him yesterday and . . ."

"Do you mean they've caught the real thief?" Whitney interrupted, her voice squeaking with excitement.

"Yes, the FBI arrested a woman named Jerri Jones and her boyfriend trying to board a plane for Brazil. The bonds were in their luggage. Mr. Greenwald also wanted me to tell you he's already picked out another assignment for you when you're done here."

Morgan paused, clearing his throat. "Whitney, there aren't words enough to thank you for what you've done. You saved my store thousands and thousands of dollars of loss. I owe you more than I can ever repay." Morgan chuckled suddenly. "But I do have an idea how I can clear at least part of that debt." His glance shifted to Bradford. "You do intend to make an honest woman of her, don't you?"

"What a question! Of course I plan to make an honest woman of Whitney, just as quickly as we can get a marriage license and find a preacher. I hope you'll be my best man." Bradford walked over to her again. "This isn't exactly the time or place I'd intended to ask you this, but you will marry me, won't you, my love?"

His expression spoke so eloquently of his love that tears flooded her eyes. With his handkerchief he mopped them gently away. "I certainly didn't think asking you to marry me would make you cry. Maybe I'd better withdraw the question," he teased, dropping a kiss on the tip of her nose.

"You do and I'll never take another shower with you!" she whispered. The laughter faded from her eyes. "Brad-

Love's Suspect 175

ford, there's nothing in the world that would make me happier than marrying you. I love you."

His possessive kiss, her willing response, sealed the vow. After several moments, Morgan interrupted, "I have a suggestion to make. Why don't you continue this nonsense later . . . in Paris?"

"Paris!" Whitney gasped.

"Yes, you heard me. I'd like to thank you by giving you two a honeymoon in Paris. And if by chance you have a little extra time you can shop some of the couture collections for Stanringham's."

"Always thinking of business, aren't you, boss?"

"No, not always." Morgan reached behind his desk and lifted up a box. "For example, this has nothing to do with business. After the phone call about Eddie's training in the navy came through I had time to do a little planning of my own. Paris is cold in November," he commented, walking toward Whitney. After placing the long box in her lap he went to the door. "I'd hate for our vice-president's wife to catch cold. Oh, I almost forgot, there's a bottle of champagne waiting for you in your office, Bradford. Take it home. I'm sure you can think of something to celebrate tonight." With a wink he walked out of the office, leaving them alone.

"Open the box," Bradford urged. "If I know the boss's mind you're going to like his surprise."

"Bradford!" she gasped, burrowing through the tissue paper, then holding up the lynx coat with the sable collar. "Is it really mine?"

"Well, you did say you liked lynx, didn't you? I'm sure Morgan feels you've earned that, and a lot more."

Bradford leaned over, then grinned. "Hmmm, lynx—this is going to be even better than an Oriental carpet," he chuckled, stroking the fur suggestively.

"You're not going to put my coat on the floor!"

"Want to bet?"

VELVET GLOVE

An exciting series of contemporary novels of love with a dangerous stranger.

Starting in July

THE VENUS SHOE Carla Neggers 87999-9/$2.25
Working on an exclusive estate, Artemis Pendleton becomes embroiled in a thirteen-year-old murder, a million dollar jewel heist, and with a mysterious Boston publisher who ultimately claims her heart.

CAPTURED IMAGES Laurel Winslow 87700-7/$2.25
Successful photographer Carolyn Daniels moves to a quiet New England town to complete a new book of her work, but her peace is interrupted by mysterious threats and a handsome stranger who moves in next door.

LOVE'S SUSPECT Betty Henrichs 88013-X/$2.25
A secret long buried rises to threaten Whitney Wakefield, who longs to put the past behind her. Only the man she loves has the power to save—or destroy her.

DANGEROUS ENCHANTMENT Jean Hager 88252-3/$2.25
When Rachel Drake moves to a small town in Florida, she falls in love with the town's most handsome bachelor. Then she discovers he'd been suspected of murder, and suddenly she's running scared when another body turns up on the beach.

THE WILDFIRE TRACE Cathy Gillen Thacker 88620-4/$2.25
Dr. Maggie Connelly and attorney Jeff Rawlins fall in love while involved in a struggle to help a ten-year-old boy regain his memory and discover the truth about his mother's death.

IN THE DEAD OF THE NIGHT Rachel Scott 88278-7/$2.25
When attorney Julia Leighton is assigned to investigate the alleged illegal importing of cattle from Mexico by a local rancher, the last thing she expects is to fall in love with him.

AVON PAPERBACKS

Buy these books at your local bookstore or use this coupon for ordering:

Avon Books, Dept BP, Box 767, Rte 2, Dresden, TN 38225
Please send me the book(s) I have checked above. I am enclosing $_____
(please add $1.00 to cover postage and handling for each book ordered to a maximum of three dollars). *Send check or money order*—no cash or C.O.D.'s please. Prices and numbers are subject to change without notice. Please allow six to eight weeks for delivery.

Name _____

Address _____

City _____ State/Zip _____

Velvet Glove 5-8